A Visitor For

Christmas

VIVIAN SINCLAIR

Copyright

This book is a work of fiction. Names, characters, places, and incidents are the product of the author's imagination or are used fictitiously. Any resemblance to actual events, locales, or persons, living or dead, is entirely coincidental.

Published by East Hill Books

Cover design: Vivian Sinclair Books

Cover illustrations credit:
© Paulus Rusyanto | Dreamstime.com
© Irinav | Dreamstime.com

ISBN-13: 978-1539828532
ISBN-10: 1539828530

Virginia Lovers Trilogy - contemporary romance:

Book 1 – Alexandra's Garden

Book 2 – Ariel's Summer Vacation

Book 3 – Lulu's Christmas Wish

A Guest At The Ranch – western contemporary romance

Maitland Legacy, A Family Saga Trilogy - western contemporary romances

Book 1, Lost In Wyoming – Lance's story

Book 2, Moon Over Laramie – Tristan's story

Book 3, Christmas In Cheyenne – Raul's story

Wyoming Christmas Trilogy – western contemporary romances

Book 1 – Footprints In The Snow – Tom's story

Book 2 – A Visitor For Christmas – Brianna's story

Book 3 – Trapped On The Mountain – Chris' story

Seattle Rain series - women's fiction novels

Storm In A Glass Of Water, a small town story

PROLOGUE

The boy hid in the loft, burrowed deep in the hay. The welts on his back hurt with every move he made. Some were older and not properly healed, crisscrossed by the new ones he got today. His stepfather's belt caught him on his left shoulder, on the fresh wound from the barbed wire the day before.

"Virgil," his mother's voice called.

The boy sank deeper into the hay. His ma was powerless against her husband. She tried once to defend him and it enraged Virgil's stepfather and made the beating worse. Since then, she'd never tried again.

"Virgil," she called louder. "He's not here," she reported outside and left closing the barn doors.

Later, much later, after midnight, when no one was around, Virgil made his way down the ladder, tiptoeing carefully. He said good-bye to the horse he'd raised from birth and which was to be sold next day, he ruffled the hair of the barn cat, and patted the two cows in the stalls.

When he was ready to leave, he saw a small bundle near the door. Two clean shirts, a pair of woolen socks, and seventeen wrinkled one-dollar bills. It was all his mother could hide from her husband.

Virgil was grateful for this. It was better than nothing. It was his inheritance, or all he was ever going to get.

Slowly, he stepped outside and made his way into the dark night, leaving behind the Montana ranch that had been the pride of his father and before him, of his ancestors. He was twelve years old.

CHAPTER 1

It was that time of year again. The beginning of December. The ranch house was decorated with greenery, lights in all the windows and strings along the edge of the roof. Inside, a majestic fir tree in the bow window of the family room sported all the decorations that had been hidden in the attic for generations. Even the bunkhouse was gifted with a smaller tree and the barn, ornate with multicolored lights, had a huge red bow hung on top of the doors. All the cowboys were walking around whistling and humming merry carols. All, except Virgil.

He was not a Scrooge. Usually, Virgil liked Christmas just fine. This year however, it brought back painful memories of his hopeless, lost love. A year ago at Christmas, Brianna Gorman, his Boss' sister had run away with a no-good cowboy from a neighboring ranch. At first, Virgil didn't believe she just left, abandoning the ranch where she grew up and her family. Oh, he knew she didn't care about him. After all, he was just a poor,

3

simple cowboy, not very handsome and certainly no smooth talker like the oily man she'd left with. She told Virgil many times that he meant nothing to her. But still, he waited, hoping she'd realize the man she chose was not worthy of her. Hoping she'd see she made a mistake and came back.

As the months went by, one after the other, his hope withered, like an unattended flame. Now it was almost extinguished.

In the kitchen, the music was playing at full blast, "Jingle bells, jingle bells…" and in front of the stove, Lottie, the Boss' wife was stirring in a large pot, moving in rhythm with the song. The flavors of garlic and herbs from the beef stew were almost overpowering the vanilla and cinnamon from the many cakes and cookies Lottie was baking continuously this time of year.

The smell alone was so enticing that it could break a man's determination to do what needed to be done. Sighing, Virgil grabbed an almond and poppy seed muffin, his favorite; Lottie baked them especially for him. They were on a platter near the snickerdoodle cookies that Angel, the mountain man, liked so much.

Wrapping another muffin in a napkin, to savor later, Virgil made his way toward the Boss' office. He knocked briefly and entered his Boss' private space, with all-around shelves bending under the load of old, leather bound books, mixed with newer paperbacks and spiral binders of various sizes. Virgil inhaled the familiar smell of leather and cigars smoked years ago by generations of less health-conscious ranchers.

Tom Gorman was frowning at his computer screen and absently waved at Virgil to sit down. Finally, he raised his eyes. "Ah, Virgil. Just the man I wanted to talk to." Looking at him, Tom noticed that something was wrong with his man. "What happened? Tell me."

"It's time for me to go, Boss," Virgil said with sadness.

Tom didn't pretend he didn't understand. "Where would you go? Do you have plans?"

Virgil shook his head. "No. I figured I could go south, to a warmer climate, Oklahoma, Texas. Someone will need a cowboy with a strong back."

"Listen, Virgil. You know I appreciate and respect you. Hank is telling me that he wants to retire and I intended to make you foreman. What do you say?"

"Why me? Why not your brother, Chris?"

"Chris is good and hard-working, but he prefers working with horses, being out on the range, not organizing and giving orders."

"True," Virgil agreed. He paused and placed the napkin on the desk. Unwrapping the muffin, he broke it in two and gave Tom half.

Tom accepted the offering, ate his half in two bites. "Good muffin. Are there any of the pink cupcakes left in the kitchen?"

"I think so. Lottie is in a frenzy of cooking. You'd think Christmas is tonight, not in four weeks."

"Yeah," Tom's face softened thinking of his wife. "She is a natural-born nurturer."

"There is no other like her. I'll miss her and her cooking. And the boys." The boys were Lottie's children from the first marriage, now adopted by Tom.

"They adore you. They follow you around like

two little puppies," Tom said. "You are practically part of this family, Virgil."

"You don't know how much this means to me, Boss. I've never had a family since my Dad died when I was six. I was just a lone drifter."

The door opened and Lottie came in carrying a plate with two huge roast beef sandwiches and a plate with chocolate chip cookies freshly baked. She placed them on Tom's desk. "You two can't decide the fate of the world without having some sustenance. Here is your lunch." Tom pulled her down in his lap and gave her a fleeting kiss. His eyes promised more for later in the privacy of their room. Laughing, Lottie returned to the kitchen.

Seeing the obvious love between the two, made Virgil more determined to leave. "What can I do, Boss? I waited a year hoping Brianna would come to her senses and return. I should have known that she is too stubborn and too proud to admit she made a mistake. Besides, it's pointless. Even if she came home, there is no hope for me. It's not like I changed into Prince Charming over night. I'm still my ugly self."

Virgil was not exactly ugly, although Tom was not an expert in masculine beauty, but his face was rather homely. If you added to that the fact that he wore his heart on a sleeve and his love for Brianna was not a secret, then it was no wonder that Brianna didn't take him seriously and was annoyed by his attention.

Women were a mystery for Tom and he thanked his lucky stars that he had found such a treasure of a wife like Lottie. Tom didn't understand why his sister could not appreciate Virgil who was hard-working and honest, not to mention tall and well-built. "Listen, there is something that you don't know. When Brianna was eighteen she fell hard for a handsome, but lazy cowboy, who had been hired for the summer at our ranch."

"Yes, I know," Virgil replied.

"I bet you do. The Gorman siblings are famous for falling in love with the wrong people. It's common knowledge in these parts."

"Not really, but the cowboys talk at the bunkhouse of this and that."

A VISITOR FOR CHRISTMAS

Tom laughed. "Worse than gossiping old women. I know. Back to our story. This cowboy dared to come to my old man to tell him that he was willing to go away and leave Brianna behind, for a price. Frankly, I think he intended to do this anyhow, but he figured the old man was gullible enough to pay. He didn't know my old man very well. Dear Dad not only didn't pay, but also chased him away with his whip, a trait he got from his friend and neighbor, Maitland. To talk and argue with people while cracking his whip on the side."

When Virgil looked at him horrified, Tom explained, "No, he didn't use it on people. It was used only to strengthen his arguments. It was all for show. Although, I wondered if on that particular occasion, he was not tempted to flog the scoundrel. Anyhow, this reinforced his opinion that Brianna is not able to take care of herself and that the land needed protection from such an unfortunate situation."

"Brianna is perfectly able to take care of herself," Virgil argued on behalf of the woman he loved.

"You'd think so, but look what happened again.

Another rogue came along and Brianna fell for him.
After the old man died, the will was read by Dad's
lawyer. Hearing that she got no part of the land, only a
large sum of money and with Dad's message that he
hoped this will help her find a worthy husband, Brie left
in a huff. So she didn't hear another small proviso our
Dad wrote in his will. Even the money willed to Brianna
cannot be used unless I approve it."

"This is really insulting to Brianna."

Tom nodded. "I thought so too, at the time. Now,
I'm not so sure. You see, it's true that I had no
communication with Brianna since she left a year ago.
But in the spring, she contacted the lawyer to withdraw
her money."

"All of it?"

"Yep, all of it. And trust me, it was quite a lot of
money. According to the proviso in the will, the lawyer
asked me what to do. I agreed to her demand only if she
came home to talk to me. I am her brother after all and
she must know I care about her."

"Still it would be humiliating to return home

asking for the money that is hers," Virgil observed, ever
so loyal to Brianna.

"Just as well she didn't come. In autumn, she
tried to have this proviso annulled arguing that she was a
thirty-year-old woman and able to make decisions on her
own. No luck here as the law is very clear – a man can
write in his will whatever he wants. Unless he is not
sound of mind, his will is valid."

"Do you know anything else about her?" Virgil
asked.

"I asked TJ Lomax, the private investigator from
Laramie, to keep tabs on her. Last I heard, she was in
Denver working in a restaurant."

"I hope not cooking." Brianna was famous for her
burnt meals, before Lottie had moved in to take over the
kitchen.

"No, not cooking or they would have fired her
immediately. She was hostess or waitress or something
like that. My point is, I know my sister. She needs to sit
on a horse and ride free on the range, not to be cooped up
all day in a smelly restaurant. I'm sure whatever love

there was between her and that cowboy, has since vanished. It always does in such cases when there is no money. And city life is not for Brianna. She'll be back soon, mark my word. If you would only wait a few more months…"

Virgil thought about it. It was tempting, oh, so tempting. But in the end, there was no happy ending for him. "No, even if Brianna returns home, it doesn't mean she is in love with me. Let's face it. I'm not her ideal of a perfect man."

"No man is perfect, Virgil. What you have to do is to ask Lottie from time to time what would impress my crazy sister. She'll give you good advice. Otherwise, who knows what women consider perfect?"

Virgil shook his head. "Even if she were to look at me more favorably, she will never love me. I'd be miserable loving her as I do and she - she'd feel trapped with a man who is not her first choice. Can you understand this, Tom?"

Of course, Tom understood. He, himself had been in love most of his adult life with a beautiful woman who was his girlfriend because she found no one better, but who considered him dull and boring. Falling in love with Lottie had been like freeing himself from invisible chains. Could he deny Virgil the same chance? "Tell you what, it's Christmastime. No one should spend it alone. Stay with us until January and then decide what you want to do. Besides, Lottie wouldn't allow you to leave before spending Christmas with us. She is preparing a huge celebration, gifts for everybody, singing carols, a lot of food and fun."

Taking the last cookie from the plate, Virgil nodded. "Very well. And thank you for everything."

CHAPTER 2

It was official. This morning Tom Gorman marched to the bunkhouse and told all the cowboys there - the few that remained at the ranch in December – that Virgil Townsend was the new foreman of the Diamond G ranch. Hank had decided to take it easy because his old leg wound was painful.

The Boss had told Virgil of this change the day before, but Virgil thought it was only an idea for the future. Too bad it happened right when he had decided that it was time for him to move on, to leave this ranch and all the sad memories of the woman he loved and who went away. It was time for him to turn a new page in his life.

Still, he was impressed by his Boss' announcement. Tom had told him often that he appreciated him, but Virgil didn't think he'd be trusted with the responsibility of running the ranch. Imagine, Virgil Townsend, runaway kid from Montana, with not much to his name, used mostly for his strong back, but derided for his curiosity, he was foreman to one of the largest ranches this side of Wyoming. Go figure!

Still shaking his head Virgil entered the kitchen, where Lottie, the Boss' wife was singing along with the radio: "Have yourself a merry little Christmas…" The kitchen smelled of all sorts of tempting aromas, from garlic and herbs to vanilla and cinnamon. All the cowboys adored Lottie, not only because she was a great cook, but also because of her cheerful and caring nature, mothering them, making them feel that they mattered, each and every one of them.

"I'm going to Laramie on some errands, Miss Lottie. Do you need anything from town?" Virgil asked, examining the platter filled with some very thin cookies.

"Yes, please Virgil. Could you drop this package with the school secretary?" Lottie was a math teacher at the local junior-high school. "And could you please go to the Cowgirl Yarn shop on East Lewis Street to pick up some yarn from there. I already ordered it yesterday. You just need to pick it up. It's for Angel's new woolen red sweater. You know how much he likes red." Lottie looked at him anxiously. "Am I too demanding, Virgil? I know I should have gone myself, but I have the roast beef in the oven and the apple pie is ready to go in."

Lottie was another soul plagued by insecurity, just like Virgil himself. He hastened to assure her, "You're not demanding Miss Lottie. How can you think so? Don't you know we are all happy to help you the best we can? You just take care of that roast beef and we are happy to do your bidding."

Lottie beamed at him. "Thank you, Virgil. Here, I made some lunch for you to tide you over until you come back." She placed a large package in his hands, enough to feed a whole army or to supply him to go to Antarctica and back. "And would you like to taste these freshly baked cookies? It's a French recipe I found online and I just experimented with it today." Lottie pointed at the platter.

Virgil took a cookie from the platter. It was paper thin. Too bad. He liked his cookies plump and moist. Gingerly, he bit from it. It melted in his mouth. He closed his eyes in order to savor the taste. He ate the rest quickly and picked up another. "It's divine, like everything you bake, Miss Lottie," he said between bites of cookie.

"It's a simple recipe, mainly butter and sugar and a handful of raisins."

"Great." With regret, Virgil turned away from the tempting cookies. "I have to go now."

After dropping Lottie's papers at school, Virgil drove to the veterinary clinic to talk to Tristan Maitland, the best veterinarian in all southeastern Wyoming. Lately, it was more and more difficult for Tristan to visit the neighboring ranches because he was extremely busy at the clinic. He had hired four other doctors and he expanded his clinic with more cage and stall space for sick or abandoned animals.

Virgil parked his truck in front and made his way in.

"Hey, Trish," he called the vet's assistant. "Call me when Tristan is available, please." Then he wandered to the back of the clinic where two men were unloading a sick cow from a trailer. He knew one of them vaguely, so he gave them a hand to coax the animal out and to get it inside the clinic into one of the empty stalls. Then he turned to go back in the waiting room when he bumped into another person.

"Excuse me," he said, clutching her arms to steady her. The woman had short brown hair and big blue eyes. She looked at him and her eyes lit up with pleasure. Truth to be told, Virgil had never in his life had this reaction from a woman looking at him. His homely face was met with indifference at best. Now, this was a pleasant change.

"Virgil, is it you? I can't believe it. I went to Parker's ranch a few months ago and they told me that you moved to a neighboring place." The woman's eyes sparkled. She had beautiful eyes, although the rest of her was average. She looked familiar, but he didn't know where to place her. "You don't remember me, do you? I'm Maggie, Maggie Anders. We met two years ago briefly, under very unfortunate circumstances, when my stepbrother wanted to involve me in his unlawful actions on the Maitland land. I didn't want to go with you then, but you were very gentle and understanding toward the scared kid that I was then."

Now he knew. "Maggie Anders. It's good to see you again. What have you been doing all this time?"

"This and that. I could tell you more if…" She looked at her watch. "I'll take a lunch break soon. Would you like to come with me? I know an excellent diner, with cheap prices and great food."

Virgil thought of the lunch prepared by Lottie that waited for him in his truck, then looked into Maggie's expectant blue eyes. What could he say? "I'd love to come." Maybe he needed some other socializing than with a bunch of rowdy cowboys. Maggie was definitely an improvement. At least she was pleasant to look at.

Virgil talked to Tristan Maitland briefly, picked up his prescription for cattle colic, and went outside to wait for Maggie.

"Am I late?" she asked climbing in the passenger's seat of Virgil's truck. She wore a soft blue cap, made from a fuzzy yarn like the ones used by Lottie and an assorted scarf that made her eyes more intensely blue.

Maggie guided him to a small diner nearby. It was modest, with Formica tables, but clean and family oriented. They both ordered the daily special of meatloaf with mashed potatoes and gravy. It was surprisingly good, just as Maggie said.

"You know, I looked for you. I was disappointed when I could not find you at Parker's ranch. Why did you leave? I thought you liked it there." Maggie said, pausing with the hot coffee cup in the air.

"I liked it fine, but after Raul Maitland took over, some of the older cowboys left or retired, including Gimpy Fred, our foreman. Maitland brought a new team of ranch hands and his trusted foreman, Lucky."

"You didn't get along with them?"

Virgil hesitated, looking outside through the window decorated with Christmas ornaments and lights. "I did, for the most part, but they were all pals from their earlier Montana days and I was the odd man out." That and the fact that one look at Tom Gorman's sister Brianna and he was smitten. But some things are better left unsaid if a man wanted to maintain his dignity.

"Do you like it better here?" Maggie asked him. "Who's your foreman?"

Still contemplating the rare snowflakes waltzing through the air outside, Virgil opened his mouth to explain that Hank was a good man to work with. Then he remembered that ... Hank was not the man in charge at Diamond G ranch. Not anymore. "I am," he answered finishing the phrase in his mind, 'foreman of the Diamond G ranch'.

"You are foreman? Get out!" Maggie exclaimed surprised and happy for him. "That's a big ranch. Good for you, Virgil."

Call him vain, but he didn't add that Tom promoted him only this morning. "How about you, Maggie?"

"I looked for you to thank you, Virgil. Two years ago, I was confused and angry. My stepbrother went to jail and almost dragged me there with him. I was alone and at almost twenty, I had no skills, no plans for the future, nothing. You have been so patient and understanding and explained that I can get my GED certificate and do what I want with my life." She touched his hand over the table.

It was nice. Not earth-shattering or bell ringing, but it was nice to feel a soft woman's touch. Maybe he was starved for a human contact, - not sex, although that was nice too and quite infrequent for Virgil – but to feel another body's warmth near him in a cold winter night. That was nice.... Maybe he was getting old and maudlin.

"Anyhow, I followed your advice and I passed the tests and got my GED," Maggie continued, still holding Virgil's hand. "I worked here and there what I could find. Now I'm a helper at the veterinarian clinic. I do everything, from receptionist to calming and holding the animals for the vets' examination to cleaning the cages and the stalls."

Virgil, who had done his share of cleaning the stalls in the barn and was often still doing it, wrinkled his nose. "Hmm, not my most favorite activity."

"I love it. Not cleaning the cages, but I love working with animals. I take classes at the Eastern Wyoming College and plan to get an associate degree in Veterinary Technology. This is why I wanted to thank you, Virgil. You made me believe in myself, believe that if I want I can do it. Be focused and have a plan."

"That's good," he said, thinking that perhaps he needed to have a plan too, like Maggie here, and not drift from one day to another.

"Virgil, do you have a girlfriend?" Maggie asked shyly, looking at him from under her long eyelashes.

The question was so unexpected, it took Virgil by surprise. "A girlfriend? Me? Who would look everyday at my ugly face?" he joked. "No, I don't."

"I think your face has a lot of character," she said cupping his cheek with her warm palm. "I want to see you again, you know, like dating. Next weekend. Think about it. Here, this is my phone number." She pushed her cell phone toward him. When he didn't do anything, too stunned to move, she wrote the number on a paper napkin. "Here. Now, I have to run back to the clinic. You don't have to give me a ride. It's close. I'll wait for your call." Having said this, Maggie bent and brushed his mouth with hers. With a mischievous twinkle in her eyes, she twirled and ran outside.

He had a date. Imagine that!

He remained sitting there at the table by the window, looking at the occasional snowflakes, listening to the Christmas music, and sipping the last of his already cold coffee.

He had one last stop before heading home. The Cowgirl Yarn shop to pick up the red yarn for Angel's sweater.

He parked his truck in a small parking lot nearby and walked to the store. He was deep in thought, still processing all that happened to him today. He stopped at the corner, waiting to cross the street. He looked to his left, where a car was approaching. After it went by, Virgil advanced to cross the street, when he heard an engine being revved behind him. Instincts of a lifetime working with animals made him step back fast. A rusty dark truck coming from behind accelerated instead of braking and turned right around the corner, fast, in fact cutting the corner, right on top of the boardwalk, where Virgil had stood before. He was not hit, but the strong airflow created by the speed of the truck or maybe his own instinct of preservation threw him to the ground.

"Are you hurt, mister?" a young man came out from a store. "I've seen it all. People here drive like maniacs, or maybe it was another drunken cowboy."

Dazed, Virgil picked himself up and assured the man he was fine. Another drunken cowboy probably. Yet, the instant when he had heard the car gunning, he had known that it was not a drunken cowboy. It was the conscious act of a person who knew well what he was doing. The sudden acceleration proved the intent.

But who would want to harm Virgil? He was poor as a church mouse and in the grand scheme of life, he was not important enough to bother anybody.

Shaking his head, Virgil walked to the yarn shop.

CHAPTER 3

Still shaken by the earlier incident, Virgil entered the small yarn shop. Six older ladies, most of them white haired, were gathered around a table covered with patterns and colorful yarn. None of them looked like the proverbial cowgirl from the firm's sign. The ladies stopped knitting and talking and looked at him with various degrees of curiosity and surprise. He'd interrupted a hen party.

Finally, one of them rose and said, "If you have a delivery for the frame store, it's next door."

Now, Virgil understood the sense of feeling like an elephant in a China store. "No. I…I'm here to pick up a parcel. Some yarn."

The lady smiled at him. "Ah, I see. For your wife."

Virgil twisted his Stetson in his hands. "No. For my Boss's wife."

"I see," she repeated and exchanged quick looks with the others. Women had this habit of understanding each other without talking. She nodded. "Yes. It's Christmastime and yarn is a nice gift."

"It's for Angel," he added, still twisting his hat.

"Ah, how nice. A nice name for a nice woman, I'm sure." She looked again at the others who nodded.

"Angel is the mountain man," Virgil tried to clarify, only to see some confusion among the ladies like they were not talking the same language. What could he say? "He likes red; I don't know why. Me, I'm partial to blue," he continued his explanations.

"What about the Boss' wife?"

"What about her? She's the one knitting. She needs the yarn."

This seemed to bring back the smiles and the nodding. "What color do you think she might like?" she asked him.

These ladies, nice as they were, were batty. "Red. Didn't I say so? Lottie is knitting a red sweater for Angel."

"Lottie? Lottie Donovan? Why didn't you say so?" She went to the back of the store and came with a parcel. Then she picked several skeins of a sky-blue yarn and wrapped them as well. "Here, these are for Lottie."

"Thank you, ma'am. And it's Gorman now. Lottie Gorman. Boss would tan my hide if I didn't correct you."

"Of course, she married that handsome boy who was in love with Parker's eldest girl," she said.

"The one with a singing voice, who married Maitland's adopted son," another one added helpfully.

"Now that is a handsome man," a white haired lady sighed. She looked old enough to be Virgil's grandmother.

"Who? The adopted son?" Another one cupped her hand over her ear to hear better.

"No, Wilma. I was talking about Elliott Maitland. He's only seventy, if he's a day, you know."

At this point, Virgil tried to back away from the store, like a bull out of its pen.

"What about you young man, what is your name?" the owner lady asked.

"Virgil. I'm Virgil Townsend," he answered.

"Virgil, you may come here anytime you want to learn to knit. It's a very useful skill. We can teach you in no time at all. Are you married?"

"No, ma'am."

This seemed to cheer the ladies even more than the idea to teach him the intricacies of the art of knitting.

"Wilma, wasn't your cousin's daughter unmarried. Perhaps we could..."

"My neighbor's niece is a very nice, educated girl and..."

Clutching tightly the two parcels, Virgil left the store as quietly as he could, leaving them debating which girl was best for him.

Wow! What a day, he thought, wiping his brow of perspiration and letting the cold air cool his heated cheeks.

Once back at the ranch, Virgil entered the kitchen and deposited the parcels in Lottie's hands.

"Thank you, Virgil," Lottie smiled at him. "It's almost dinner time. You should go wash and call the

29

others."

The kitchen smelled very appetizing, but Virgil was preoccupied by his own thoughts. He took a seat at the table and Lottie aware of his strange mood, placed a mug with hot tea in front of him and waited for him to speak.

"I loved Brianna from the first moment I saw her. She was this …luminous face in my hard life."

Lottie patted his shoulder. "Virgil, that is so poetic."

"Yes, well, she didn't feel equally poetic toward me. Not that I blame her. I see myself every morning in the mirror when I shave myself. I know I'm not handsome or a smooth-talker to charm the ladies. But I hoped that at least she'll see the honesty of my feelings compared to the others' empty words."

"I'm sorry. Is that why you wanted to leave us? Tom told me."

He nodded, absently drinking the tea. "I've waited and waited for her to see the truth and to come back. Tom said she was no longer with that cowboy, Joe

Brown or whatever his name was. Maybe she discovered the truth about him, but she didn't come back. So, one morning I woke up and knew that I can't go on hoping like an idiot that she'll change. I knew I had to move on with my life, away from here, where everything reminds me of her. I am a drifter after all, Miss Lottie. Never meant to have a home and a family of my own."

"No, Virgil. It's not true. If you feel you have to go, then you have to. But you will always have a home with us here. My boys think the sun rises with you. They love you so much. You are the uncle they follow around. They'll be very upset if you go. And Tom...Tom relies on you for everything on this ranch."

Virgil smiled at Lottie. "I know he doesn't want me to leave. Can you believe he named me foreman?"

"Of course I believe it. Tom told me that this entire year you were in charge of the ranch. Naming you foreman officially was only a formality."

He looked at her surprised. "I've always pitched in to help Hank, but..."

"You organized the spring round-up. The newly

hired hands came to you in the morning to ask what needed to be done that day. You were the one making decisions. Tom and Hank have been talking about this for a long time and naming you foreman was not a spur-of-the-moment idea to convince you to stay."

"Oh, Miss Lottie, I don't know what to say. It's really nice to be appreciated."

She patted his arm again. "You are very much appreciated here at the Diamond G ranch. You're a good man, Virgil. Think about all this and make the decision that is right for you. And... remember that you deserve to be happy and there is always hope in life, even when it looks like only a miracle would help."

He nodded. "Thank you for listening to me and for the encouraging words." He made no move to go. "There is more. Can I tell you?"

"You can tell me anything you want. I'm a good listener and we're in luck, the boys are not here, yet."

"Well, I met this girl, you see....," he said frowning at his now empty teacup.

Lottie plopped down on a chair near him, her

smile widening. "Frankly, I've been waiting for a long time to hear you say this."

Surprised, he raised his eyes at her. "Why?"

"A good man needs a nice girl to make his life better."

"I'm not sure she's the one, Miss Lottie. I met her two years ago, when her stepbrother dragged her into one of his nefarious schemes. He's in jail now, and she's managed to turn her life around, taking her GED and attending community college, planning to become a veterinary technician. She is determined and I admire her for this."

"What's she doing now?"

"She works as a helper at Maitland Veterinary clinic. I almost envy her for knowing what she wants and having the guts to go for it. Compared to her I feel like I'm drifting aimlessly through life. I worked in construction for a while and the money was good, but I yearned for the open spaces on the range and I looked for work as a cowboy."

"You're doing well, Virgil. You're doing what

you like. Not many people can say this. But back to the girl, do you like her?"

He shrugged. "She's pretty, although not picture beautiful like Brianna. There is no other woman like Brianna. Maggie's nice. There are no bells and whistles when I'm with her, but I like her. She has a soft brown short hair and incredibly big blue eyes with long eyelashes. What's amazing is that she was looking for me at Parker's ranch and she wants to go on a date with me. I don't know why. I'm nothing to look at and I don't have two pennies to my name. But there you have it – she wants to date me."

"And how do you feel about going on a date with her?"

He thought about it and scrunched up his nose. "Frankly, I've never been on a real date before. Of course I went with the boys into town on Saturday nights to some seedy bars to have a beer and occasionally I met there a lonely woman in need of company, but that is not a date, is it?"

"No, it's not."

"I feel strange to go out with a woman who is not Brianna, not that she would ever agree to go on a date with me. It's not easy to be constantly mocked by the woman you love. I shrug it off, but it hurts. This girl is nice and she likes me. But how can I date her when I still love Brianna? I don't want to be dishonest with her. What if I can't return her feelings, because my twisted heart still wants Brianna? What should I do?"

"I think you should go out with her, tell her the truth, and give her a chance. You will know in your heart if she is the one."

"Ah, Miss Lottie, you think she is."

"No, I don't. What I think is that it's high time you got over the runaway Brianna and see if a real woman is not better and exactly what you need instead of an infatuation that will get you nowhere. Or, if perhaps there was more than infatuation you felt for Brianna, and it was the passion of your life. Only you can decide this. But you have to give this woman and yourself a chance."

He nodded. "All right, I will. Anyhow, she seems very determined in everything she does."

"There you go. Just follow her lead and see where it takes you."

CHAPTER 4

Brianna Gorman was coming home after being away for almost one year. She knew people in town were saying that she had lost her head again to a handsome cowboy, just like she did when she was eighteen. It didn't matter to her. Then and now, she liked the man, but she had agreed to leave with him because she needed to discover what else was out there in the world, to see more, to learn more.

The first time, she didn't go anywhere because her father chased the greedy scoundrel from the ranch. Now she got to Denver. Unfortunately, she had to tell Joe, as he called himself, that she owned no part of the Diamond G ranch. That sent him flying into the night literally, after a failed attempt to make her brother release her inherited funds.

Instead of returning home defeated, she chose to stay. And she never regretted it. She got a job at a fancy restaurant. First as waitress, then as hostess, and three month ago as assistant manager. She loved her job and the responsibilities that came with it. She discovered she was good at making quick decisions in unexpected situations.

She rented a small studio apartment in trendy Stapleton and made several good friends. She enjoyed the artistic life in the city. In her free time, she explored downtown, visiting museums, art galleries, and libraries. She also hiked on the many available trails. It was a wonderful experience, although at times she missed her family ranch and the open spaces of Wyoming. One day, she woke up knowing it was time to return home. It was December and she wanted to celebrate Christmas with her family. She missed her brothers, Lottie, and her two little boys. She was homesick.

So here she was, standing in front of the ranch house where she was born, with all her belongings loaded up in her truck. The house was decorated with light strings and had a large wreath on the front door adorned with a huge red bow.

Oh, how much she'd missed them all!

Brianna looked around with curiosity. Two

cowboys were talking in front of the barn. She didn't know them. She admired the tall, strongly built one, dressed in a new shearling coat. He had his back at her and was talking to the shorter man, who was nodding in understanding. The tall one had a commanding presence, while the other one had a more deferential attitude. Then the shorter cowboy mounted his horse and rode away.

It seemed that Tom had hired new people. And what interesting characters. The tall man turned slowly and looked at her. He took it all in, her dusty old truck, stuffed with all her things, and her, standing nearby, in her pink parka, so out of place at the ranch. His eyes were inscrutable and his face gave nothing away.

Brianna's jaw dropped when recognition struck. "Virgil?"

He touched the brim of his hat in salute. "Brianna." No welcoming words. No smile on his face. Then he turned away and made his way to the bunkhouse.

She had a hard time reconciling this imposing figure, hard and unsmiling, with the old Virgil, who was always ready to do anybody's bidding, eager to please, and who followed her around like a lovesick puppy.

She shook her head and entered the house. Attracted by the incredible aroma from the kitchen, Brianna went straight there. There was cheerful Christmas music from an old radio and Lottie was singing along, while decorating a cake.

"Mmm, chocolate cake. Whose birthday is it today?"

Startled, Lottie dropped the icing knife on the table. "Brianna, you came back home." She clapped her hands, and then rushed to embrace her, laughing and crying and talking all at once. "Tom and the boys will be so happy to see you. I wish I'd known you were coming. I only have lasagna today."

Brianna laughed. "I love lasagna, especially when I'm not the one who made it."

But Lottie was not listening. "Oh, what a nice surprise. Imagine how happy Tom will be."

Brianna swiped some icing from the knife. "Good. The cake is very festive."

A VISITOR FOR CHRISTMAS

"I made it for Cory. He is a young man hired by Tom this summer. The poor dear. He had just finished high school when his mother died in a car accident. He is all alone in the world and he is staying with us for Christmas. He said his mother used to make him chocolate cake. So I thought to make one today."

Brianna looked at Lottie. "What are you carrying there? Triplets?" she said gently patting Lottie's burgeoning stomach.

"Just one big boy."

"I bet Tom is beside himself with pride and joy."

Lottie laughed. "We both are. And the boys too. They imagine their new brother will be born already grown and of their age, so they'd have someone else to play with." She pulled Brianna to sit down. "But enough about us. Tell me how you are. You look very …citified and sophisticated. I think this adventure was good for you, regardless of how much it worried Tom. I'm glad you came back." She looked at Brianna, hesitating to speak.

"What?"

"I was afraid you left partly because of me. Because I married Tom and took over the house... well, sort of," she confessed, biting her lower lip in anxiety.

Brianna took her hand. "No way. How could you think that? On the contrary, I was happy that Tom married you. You make him happy and that's what is important. As for the house, you can take over it with my blessing. Not to mention that every soul on this ranch is happy that you took over. It's funny, but I rented a tiny studio apartment in Denver and I enjoyed decorating it. I bought silly things like pillows, candles, and flowers. I never felt the need for that with this house. Strange, huh?"

"No, not strange at all. Your rented studio was your own, while this big house was more like a family place for everybody. It was not your personal space to make it your own. Anyhow, I hope you found what you were looking for in Denver."

"Yes, Lottie. Now I know what I want. I want to buy a place of my very own. As small or large as my inherited money will allow. I know I can make a living."

A VISITOR FOR CHRISTMAS

Lottie patted her hand. "I'm sure Tom will help with whatever you want to achieve. But why am I blabbering on. Let's go see Tom."

Tom was looking at his computer screen frowning at an invoice for some feed order he didn't recall buying. He was wearing glasses, which he had bought secretly. It was not exactly vanity, but who had ever heard of a rancher riding on the range wearing glasses. Luckily for him, he only needed them for reading.

The door opened and his darling wife Lottie stopped in the doorway. She was smiling, radiating happiness. "Tom, we have a visitor for Christmas." She stepped aside and his wayward sister came in.

"Hello, Tom. I came home," she announced simply.

He jumped from his chair and caught his sister in his arms. "You little idiot. Do you realize how scared we were for you? How could you…"

"Tom," Lottie interrupted him. "Brianna is home

now. Let's be happy."

The door opened again and Chris came in grinning. "What's this I hear? Our dear sister finally returned home."

"Chris!" Brianna went into his open arms and he caught her in a bear hug.

"I did not exactly 'hear', but I saw the truck outside and the men were talking." As usual Chris joked about his hearing impediment. "You got tired of your Denver adventure?"

She smiled looking at him so he could read her lips. "No, not at all. But I missed this ranch and our family. The Denver adventure, as you call it, accomplished two things. I saw what else is out there – and trust me, I needed the experience very much – and it proved that I can manage and live on my own."

"And now, will you be content to stay and work here on the ranch?" he asked, voicing what perhaps they all wondered.

"I have plans and I want to share them with you all, but for the moment, let's enjoy the Christmas celebration together and Lottie's lasagna."

"Oh, my lasagna," Lottie cried and flew out the door to the kitchen.

"I hope I didn't make Lottie's lasagna look and taste like one of my own meals."

Tom laughed. "You couldn't, even if it got burned. Somehow Lottie's food tastes delicious no matter what."

"Are you going to work on the ranch like you did before?" Chris asked. "You look… different."

"I know. Lottie said I look citified." Brianna laughed. "Don't worry, I have my old clothes with me and you can tell old Hank I'll report to work tomorrow."

Chris looked at Tom, who answered her. "Yes, well, about that. Hank is semi-retired. He is visiting family in Cheyenne. There have been some changes here since you left."

"Wait a minute. Then who is foreman now?"

Again Tom and Chris exchanged looks. "The best of us all, Virgil."

"Virgil? You mean 'always curious, funny man

Virgil'? You can't be serious, Tom." Brianna was stunned. "This is a big ranch, a large operation that requires a lot of coordination and you can't be everywhere Tom. This is not a joke, is it?"

"No. No joke. Virgil has been acting foreman since spring when Hank reinjured his wounded leg. Virgil hired new people and they looked to him for orders and guidance. He thought he was helping Hank, when in fact he was acting foreman. He is the best."

Brianna shook her head. "Wow! I don't know what to say. It's like we're talking about two entirely different people. The Virgil I knew was …a clown."

"That was the way you saw him. You never saw the hard-working, reliable man he is," Chris added softly, looking from Tom to Brianna to see their lips and understand what they said.

"Your opinions are your own, Brie," Tom said. "But please don't insult Virgil or try to be ironical and diminish his authority. Don't put him in a difficult position to correct you or to reply in kind. I am warning you that unless he makes a mistake that might affect the ranch, I'll side with him."

Brianna raised both hands up. "All right. I'll try not to fight with him, unless he is incapable of doing a foreman's job. I am warning you also that I'm not going to stand by and watch Virgil do some crazy thing because he is curious to see the results."

Tom smiled. "Fair enough. Now let's go eat Lottie's lasagna."

CHAPTER 5

Ever since Lottie had married Tom Gorman, it was a tradition at the ranch to serve dinner at the large farm table in the kitchen.

Brianna was curious to meet the ranch hands hired during the year she had been away. But first she wanted to say hello to Lottie's children from her first marriage, who had been adopted by Tom. "Where are the two little boys?" she asked Lottie. She had missed them.

"They were so tired from frolicking in the snow outside that I gave them a light meal and sent them both to bed. They fell asleep before I even turned off the light," Lottie explained, placing on the table freshly baked bread, smelling heavenly, and bowls full of a soup so thick and full of chunks of meat and vegetables that it looked more like a stew.

There were a few men who were staying at the ranch over Christmas. They were starting to come in for dinner. Brianna only knew Angel, the giant mountain man, usually taciturn, now whistling a well-known holiday song. He sported a hand-knitted red vest over his flannel shirt. Then came Cory, the youngster, not yet twenty, lanky and shy.

"Brianna, you know Angel. And this is Cory," Tom said by way of introduction, taking his seat at the end of the table. He was distracted by exchanging heated looks with his wife, who was placing a steaming bowl of soup in front of him. "Lottie, I told you we can serve ourselves. You are not to lift heavy things and tire yourself."

"Yes, Tom," Lottie agreed meekly, trying not to laugh. "I could certainly tire myself carrying this bowl to the table."

"Nice vest, Angel," Brianna said, glad to see the mountain man again. He was one of the few people she trusted to do things right on the range. Angel touched his vest and smiled at Lottie. Brianna continued, "...and Cory, nice to meet you," she added looking at the teenager, which prompted him to blush to the top of his ears.

The other two were Tiny Pete and Travis. The

first one was not as tiny as his name claimed. Of course, compared to the other men at the table who were tall, he was more like an average person. Still he had an inch or two over Brianna's five foot seven and he practically dwarfed short Lottie. He was joking and laughing all the time.

"We sure are lucky, ma'am, to see here not only one, but two beautiful women on this ranch. No offense Boss, but after living day in and day out looking only at other cowboys, it's a pleasure to look at such beautiful ladies at the end of the day," he said, patting his bushy moustache. He was a charmer.

"Mind your manners boys. Brianna will join us on the range," Tom warned them.

Tiny Pete was surprised. "What? Such a delicate lady will do a cowboy's work?"

Last year, Brianna would have taken exception to being called 'delicate'. But after living in Denver, she accepted it as a compliment, as it was intended.

"My sister worked for years on this ranch and she knows her way around cattle," Tom said between two spoonfuls of the delicious soup.

The second cowboy, Travis, was also called Gipsy or Champion. He was an ex-rodeo bull rider. He had won some competitions several years ago and had a collection of buckles to prove it, so he was sometimes called Champion by the others after a few beers. Gipsy was his nickname because he claimed to be a gipsy who roamed the west, never happy to remain in one place for too long. He was also quiet and more serious, only nodding at Brianna.

They were almost finished with the soup when the door opened and Virgil entered. Brianna felt a shiver of awareness down her spine that left her confused. She thought it was the frigid air that he brought in with him or the irritation she always felt at his curious nature and eagerness to please her. No worries there! He ignored her completely and took a seat near the other end of the table. He leaned toward Tom and looking at Chris so he could read his lips, he said something in a low voice for Tom's ears only.

Lottie placed a bowl of soup in front of him and

he smiled his 'thank you' over his shoulder. He kept a serious demeanor throughout the entire dinner, not looking at Brianna at all. He was not ignoring her; he acted like she was not there, like she was not special. And this made her sad for some unknown reason.

He looked... not handsome, how could Virgil be handsome... but nice, in his blue sweater over a denim shirt. He projected much more confidence than when she'd left home. So many changes had occurred in just a short year.

Meanwhile, Lottie filled the plates with lasagna. Despite being half-full with the soup, the strong aroma of garlic, basil, and tomato sauce made the men look impatiently at Cory, who was helping bring the plates to the table. The baskets were refilled with fresh bread and for a while the kitchen was quiet, while the men ate.

"Excellent meal, ma'am, thank you," Tiny Pete said, leaning back in his chair.

And then the conversation flowed again.

"I'm going to the tavern on Saturday. There is a trucker in town who said he's better at pool than me. I intend to challenge him to a game and make him buy my beer," Travis was telling Angel.

"I want to see this too," Cory said, eager to fit in with the other ranch hands. "Are you coming, Virgil?"

"He-he, Virgil has a hot date Saturday night," Tiny Pete announced, grinning under his moustache.

Brianna blinked. Virgil had a date? Surely not. It couldn't be true. Tiny Pete was mocking him. Wasn't he?

As if he'd heard her thoughts, Tiny Pete continued, "With that pretty filly who works at the vet's clinic."

"Trish?" Brianna wondered, before realizing she'd voiced her question out loud.

"Nah, Trish is old and married," Cory answered her.

Trish was barely twenty-six. How could she be old? Brianna at thirty felt positively ancient.

"Maggie is twenty or so. And mighty pretty, with eyes bluer than the Montana sky," Tiny Pete supplied more information. "Too bad she's Virgil's girlfriend or I'd consider courting her myself."

"You are a randy old goat and she'd not give you the time of day, even if she weren't Virgil's girlfriend. You'd better go for Widow Krammer," Travis told him.

"Widow Krammer is probably fifty-five," Tiny Pete protested with indignation.

"About your age, I'd say."

"You should know I just passed forty."

Lottie brought a chocolate cake to the table and that got their full attention. "I made this cake for Cory," Lottie said, looking at the young cowboy.

"What? All of it for him?" Tiny Pete frowned, touching his impressive moustache.

"No, of course not. It's for all of us. But he told me that his mother used to make chocolate cake for him, not only at special occasions, but also when she wanted to cheer him up and make him happy. I don't have her exact recipe, but I made this in her memory."

"Thank you, Miss Lottie." Cory sniffed and his eyes filled with tears. Embarrassed, he rose to leave. "Excuse me."

Tom stopped him. "Sit down, son. There is

nothing to be ashamed of, just for missing your ma. I was twenty-three when I lost my father and I cried like a baby. And I knew it was bound to happen, because he was smoking and nothing and no one could make him stop."

Relieved that no one thought him a weakling crying for his mother, Cory sat back down. Lottie cut the cake and passed around the table the plates with the sweet dessert.

"I never knew my ma," Tiny Pete said. "So young Cory, be happy that you had yours for nineteen years and have nice memories of her."

"Good cake, ma'am." Travis pushed his empty plate away. "Thank you for dinner." He rose to go.

"Here. Take this box with cookies with you to the bunkhouse to have for tonight." Lottie gave him a large box.

CHAPTER 6

Virgil looked at the dark sky. He knew in his bones that it was going to snow that afternoon. The wind was rather cutting and one of those blinding blizzards was coming.

Travis rode in, his horse's breath steaming in the frigid air. "We have trouble, Virgil. A mountain lion attacked the cattle on the east pasture and killed a young calf. I shot it, but he's not dead. He ran away, leaving behind a thin trail of blood. I didn't want to chase it farther without telling you. My cell phone had no signal there."

"Change the horse and I'll come with you. Cory, get your rifle and come with us." Virgil looked at the others. "Angel and Tiny, finish loading the feed and go spread it on the west pasture. Brianna and Chris, go help them finish faster. Come back as soon as you finish. We'll have bad weather tonight."

"No." Brianna stepped forward. "I'm not going with Angel. If you're planning to follow the cougar, then

I want to come too. I know that rocky terrain to the east very well." She became aware that the others had stopped what they were doing and there was silence in the yard. She raised her chin mutinously.

Virgil stopped arranging his saddle and turned to face her. He had the same impenetrable, unsmiling face as before. Only his eyes narrowed a little. "Brianna, you will go help Angel, Chris, and Tiny spread feed for the cattle in the west pasture and do it quickly. Or, you can go inside and join Lottie in the family room to teach you to knit. Your choice." Having said this, he mounted his horse and rode away, followed closely by Travis and Cory.

"Darn! Stubborn man." She stomped her foot in frustration. "Where is Tom?"

"Gone into town with business," Angel answered. "Come, the wagon is full. We have to ride away. And we need to do it fast, before the blizzard starts."

What could Brianna do? Muttering to herself, calling Virgil all sorts of not very flattering names, she mounted her own horse and rode after Angel. Tiny Pete was driving the wagon. He was the only one who was cheerful. Chris was looking from time to time at the ominous dark sky with low hanging clouds. Yep, he thought, a blizzard was on the way just as Virgil predicted.

Angel rode closer to Brianna. "Miss Brie, you have to understand that things are not the same as they were when you left. Hank was a very laid-back foreman. He was and is a good, trustworthy man, but he was getting older and more lax with the ranch hands. In spring, we hired this cowboy from Nevada, Bill. Hank told him to repair the fence bordering Circle M ranch. Bill supposedly went to fix the fence every morning, until one day Raul Maitland rode in and told Tom that our cattle are mixed with his own on his land. Virgil went to sort the cattle and sent two others to fix the fence. Then he drove to town where he found Bill drunk in a tavern. He fired him on the spot. Since then, he took over Hank's job. The men looked up to him and accepted his decisions. He thought he was just helping Hank, who was in pain and incapacitated by his old leg wound. In reality, Virgil has been acting as a very competent foreman for almost a year now. However, Tom officially named him foreman quite recently. And you should know Missy, it's not wise to challenge his authority. It makes him look weak in front of the men. Not that any one of them would think Virgil weak. He's proven himself strong and in control countless times. But still, I think you shouldn't contradict him in front of the men."

It was the longest speech Brianna had ever heard from the usually quiet mountain man. She liked him and respected his opinion. "I didn't mean to challenge his decision," she said. "I thought that curiosity drove him again to run straight into danger. I once saw a man attacked by an enraged, wounded cougar. Trust me, it was not a pretty sight and I had nightmares for a long time afterward. I thought it was just like Virgil to throw himself into another dangerous situation without thinking. I thought I could at least be there and warn him when he is not paying attention."

Angel pulled up his collar against the biting wind. "I see that you wanted to help and that is very nice of you, but things have changed around here. Virgil has changed. With all the responsibilities that came with the job, he matured fast. He placed his curiosity on the back burner and became a reliable man.

"But he's taking risks, like now with the wounded cougar," Brianna argued.

"Virgil will never send another man to face danger. He will do it himself. It's part of the job to ensure the men's safety and it shows the kind of man Virgil is. That's why men respect him. He'd never ask of them to do what he would not do himself."

They rode in silence for a while, and Brianna ruminated on these new facts.

"Don't worry," Angel said. "Virgil is a seasoned, experienced cowboy. He will not take unnecessary risks. He'll be fine, you'll see."

They reached the west pasture an hour later. In good weather, a strong horse could take a rider there in less than half an hour. But the constant wind made them wrap their scarves tighter and the horses pulling the wagon were slower, barely trotting forward against the wind.

They found the cattle huddled together in a dip between two crops of rocks. They felt the approaching blizzard too.

Tiny Pete handled the wagon, while the others started to spread the feed around. It took them a long time to do it, but at least they knew the cattle had a chance to survive. Another hour passed by the time Chris brought back a calf that had gotten lost and Brianna chased the others back together. Snow started falling, at first only rare flakes blown by the wind, slowly coming down more intense, swirled by the cutting wind.

"Let's hurry back. Soon we'll have a full blown blizzard," Chris shouted.

They arrived back at the ranch just in the nick of time before the blizzard developed into a dangerously strong storm. A man could get lost and freeze just by walking from the barn to the ranch house or to the bunkhouse. Ropes were tied from one place to the other as guidance in case the blizzard was truly blinding.

"Virgil is not back yet," Brianna observed

looking into the empty stall in the barn.

"He'll be fine," Angel answered unconcerned, unsaddling the horses.

Brianna marched straight inside where she found her brother in the kitchen embracing his wife. "Tom," she cried.

He jumped back like a teenager caught making out by the girl's father. "What? Brie, you gave me a heart attack. Can't you knock on the door before bursting in like the house is on fire?"

"It's not on fire, Tom, but close. Did you look outside? It's a full blown blizzard. The snowfall is so dense that you can barely see."

"I just returned from town. There was ice on the road, but my truck, old as it is, was holding up fine. The engine is tuned-up and the tires are new. So I made it back safely. Thank you for asking. Now, I'd like to kiss my wife, if you don't mind."

"Tom, do you realize Virgil, Travis, and the youngster, Cory, left this morning to follow a mountain lion that killed a calf? They are not back." Brianna paced the length of the kitchen agitated. "And I told Virgil I wanted to go with them. I know the eastern pasture better than anyone, but nooo. He had to impose his newly acquired authority. What now? We have to ride again in this awful weather to search for them."

"No, we don't," Tom answered decidedly.

"But they might be lost or in trouble. That curious idiot, Virgil, might be hurt," Brianna continued to argue.

"Since when do you care so much about Virgil?"

"I care about any man on this ranch, apparently more than you do."

"Brie, listen to me, of course I care about all of them, but I'm not going to risk more lives on a fool's errand to search in this weather. And I know Virgil. He is a very experienced cowboy and knows this land. He is smart and resourceful. I'm sure he found shelter somewhere when the blizzard started. Unfortunately, there is no cell phone signal in the east. But there are a number of shacks that are kept in good order all the time, with blankets and food all year around, in case someone gets lost. There are also natural places where he can find shelter like caves or rocks. They could even dig a makeshift place to take cover until the weather improves. Don't worry about Virgil. He'll be fine." Having said this, Tom went back to kissing Lottie.

"He'll be fine," Brianna repeated going near the window to look outside. She pressed her nose to the cold glass. It was a winter wonderland. A white curtain obscured everything. She could barely distinguish darker shapes and flickering lights where she knew the barn and the other outbuildings were.

She sighed. Virgil was a good tracker and an outdoorsman. He found shelter for sure. Why was she so concerned about what happened to him? A year ago, she would not have been worried at all. His curiosity had gotten him into a heap of trouble in the past and no one had worried about him… How sad. To get lost and to know there is no one in this world to care. The ranch hands would have gone to search for him later, but it was not the same as knowing there is at least one human being who cares. That you are important to someone. Did Virgil live like that all his life, alone and without a soul in the world to care about him?

Brianna shook her head. What silly thoughts. Did she care about Virgil? Of course she didn't. And the fact that he was not in love with her anymore was a good thing. No more shuffling his big feet, trying to say or do something to please her, no more following her around with that ugly hangdog face. But instead of cheering her up, this thought depressed her more.

What was wrong with her? It must be the weather.

The door opened and two little boys came in. They were Lottie's kids from her first marriage.

"Brianna, let me show you my Galaxy Android," Billy, the youngest cried.

Brianna remembered a long gone time, when a boy of Billy's age – he was six – would have shown his aunt his most prized possession, a wooden horse. Now it was an Android or some other electronic device. Would their ancestors be amazed by these new times, when kids play with iPads instead of wooden horses?

"Did you two little angels look ahead of time at

what Santa dropped under the tree?"

Two little faces looked innocently at her. "No, we didn't. I got this for my birthday in September," Billy said smiling at her, showing his recently missing front tooth.

Brianna opened her arms wide. "Come here you two. I missed you so much."

CHAPTER 7

Following the mountain lion was not easy. The wind had swirled the snow covering the traces. Virgil was one of the best local trackers and he had a hard time finding the trail. He dismounted and holding the horse's bridle in one hand and his rifle in the other, he pulled his scarf higher to cover his neck and face and tried to dust away, here and there, the superficial layer of snow blown by the wind.

The land looked deserted, although the wounded animal could be anywhere beyond the surrounding rocks.

"I think this is where I shot him. I'm sure here he left a thin trail of blood on the old layer of snow," Travis said looking around.

Cory was the best shooter among them, but he was no tracker. He had no idea what to look for.

There was nothing here, no traces, no blood, nothing. And to try to dust off what the wind was blowing back immediately, was pointless. Virgil was thinking he'd come on a fool's errand and turned to tell the others they should all return at the ranch before the weather worsened, when he saw at a distance a darker spot on the ground. He handed his horse's bridle and his rifle to Cory and squatted to examine the spot.

"It's blood, all right. And it's fresh. I doubt the cougar bled to death from Travis' shot. A graze on the flank doesn't bleed much. I think there was another shooter who finished him off and probably carted him away." Virgil put his glove back on and brushed the snow off a larger area. "Here. There are some faint traces of human boots." He turned around to show the others, when Travis launched at him knocking him down to the ground.

A shot echoed and the ground where Virgil had been kneeling splattered around in a spray of frozen snow, pebbles, and rocky particles.

Cory raised his own rifle and shot in the distance where he thought he'd seen a glitter above a big boulder.

Travis got up, dusted himself off, and extended a hand to Virgil who was still dazed by the fall. "Enough Cory," Travis shouted. "He rode away, whoever he was."

Cory stopped shooting. "How do you know?"

"I heard him. I have very good hearing and sight," Travis explained. "Not that it helped me become better or richer, but it saved my hide several times, like today.

"Thank you guys," Virgil said. "You saved my life. It's a novel experience for me."

"Sure. You're a good man Virgil. A better foreman than most I know. Trust me, I met some very mean people out there. This youngster," Travis pointed to Cory. "... is lucky to have you. I knew one in Texas who used to let go of the barbed wire right when I tried to wrap it around the post and nail it there. He did it on purpose."

"What did you do?" Cory asked knowing Travis was not the man to let such things pass.

"I dropped the hammer right there at his feet and left. Never looked back."

Virgil took his rifle from Cory. "All right. Let's go back. The blizzard is coming faster than I thought."

After twenty minutes of riding against the cutting

wind, the snowfall became dense and visibility was poor. They were advancing in a white ocean, without being able to distinguish any rocks or other familiar scenery. Everything was white.

Virgil stopped them. "It's bad. We can't reach the ranch. Follow me. He turned left and rode farther away from the ranch. The other two followed. From time to time, Virgil slowed down to a trot and observed the surroundings closely. The others had no idea where they were. They followed Virgil and hoped he knew better. Were they lost?

Apparently not. After another ten minutes, which seemed like ages in the frigid air that cut to the bone, they saw a small house. There was no smoke from the chimney, but whatever it was looked much better than frozen ground.

When they came closer, they saw that it was a solidly built house of stone and wood and with a fairly new roof. It had an empty barn near it, where they lead the horses.

"Who lives here?" Cory asked, unsaddling his

horse and leading it to a feeding trough.

"Virgil, you are a wizard to conjure up a shelter like this," Travis said, grabbing his saddle and leading the way to the house.

The door was unlocked and the interior of the house was as neat and clean as the barn. Virgil set his saddle down and looked around with satisfaction. "This is the old Maitland homestead. It was built over a hundred years ago. Some part of it was destroyed by a fire and rebuilt. For a while, the Old Man Maitland's younger brother, Erik lived here, or used it as his personal retreat. He owned this smaller ranch, the Morning Star ranch, but in fact he was not actively working on it. I understand he was a recluse and preferred to let the Old Man to manage both spreads."

"So nobody lives here now?" Cory asked looking around with curiosity. The house was kept in good order, but the interior looked like a picture from a Victorian magazine, a place suspended a hundred years in time.

"Not now. Three or four years ago, Tristan Maitland, the vet lived here with his son."

"I thought the vet had a large place in town, close to his clinic."

"He does now. But he lived here before marrying Judge Eleanor Maitland," Virgil explained absently, examining the provisions in the tiny kitchen space. It was well stocked.

"So the vet owns this place too?" Cory asked, looking at the old pictures on the wall.

"This place together with the Morning Star ranch is owned by Lance Maitland. Nobody knows why the Old Man adopted Raul and left him the much larger Circle M ranch." Virgil paused and scratched his head. It was a mystery that the family kept private. "The fact is Lance and Raul were raised together like brothers. Although they own different properties, the ranching operation is one business, done together." He was curious himself, but no matter how much he'd asked John Parker, all Parker said was that Old Man Maitland had been fair with all his three sons, giving each of them what they wanted. Well, Parker would say so considering his daughter Faith was married to Raul and Raul got the largest ranch. "Well, family business."

"I personally don't care who owns it," Travis said, rubbing his hands with satisfaction when he saw a tiny flame flickering from the bundle of woods he'd placed in the fireplace. "I'm grateful we are finally warm. A man can die if he is lost in a blizzard. Now, let's see to the food."

"The Maitlands keep this homestead in good condition and supplied permanently, just in case. And it's a good thing they do." Virgil looked into the package Lottie gave him before leaving. A plastic box with chicken enchiladas and one with almond and poppyseed muffins, two of them. His favorite. He placed them on the table.

"I have three huge roast beef sandwiches and brownies," Cory announced.

Travis took a seat at the square wooden table, scared and carved like it was of an age with the homestead. "Fried chicken with mashed potatoes and gravy and sugar cookies. I don't suppose we have a microwave in this Victorian paradise."

"We sure do," Virgil inclined his head toward the kitchen counter.

"Say Virge," Cory asked later, after they ate and when they were drinking hot coffee from the mugs in the kitchen. "Who do you think shot at us?"

"Not us," Travis contradicted him while lazily shuffling a deck of playing cards. "The shooter targeted Virgil specifically. Unless he intended to take us out one at a time. But I don't think so. Have you made any new enemies lately, Virgil?"

This question was bothering Virgil since they rode back in the snow. "Not that I know of. Besides I don't have anything anyone might want. No money, no beautiful wife, no top of the line car. I don't see what they would gain by eliminating me. It must have been an accident." But in the back of his mind a niggling thought kept reminding him that he had another 'accident' in Laramie, when a truck cut the corner right where he had been a second before.

"These ranches here are so large and isolated that there is often an outlaw running away or some other crazy man hiding in the most remote corners. Tom needs to know that another man is hiding on his land and that he was shooting at us."

"Will the sheriff come to look for him?" Cory asked.

Virgil shook his head. "Only if a crime had been committed. Otherwise we have to do the policing ourselves."

"Maybe the shooter envied Virgil for his beautiful girlfriend," Travis said continuing to flip his cards.

Virgil looked at him dumbstruck. "Are you nuts? Brianna doesn't give me the time of day. In fact, she can't stand me and said I'm ugly."

Travis stopped playing with his cards and gave Virgil a long look. "Oh my friend, you messed it up real well. I was not talking about our Boss' haughty sister. I was thinking of a cute girl, with short hair and big blue eyes, who works for the vet. Does it ring a bell?"

"Maggie is cute indeed, and very funny to be with. She's always joking," Cory confirmed nodding vigorously.

"Did it occur to you that all the cowboys from the neighboring ranches find too often a sick animal to present it to the vet? Just to have the opportunity to see Maggie and to hear her laugh," Travis continued. "And she wants you."

"I don't know why," Virgil said honestly. "I met her in a very difficult moment in her life two years ago. I did my best to encourage her to go on with her life, that she'd be fine. At that time, she was like a kitten hissing against everyone, scared and confused. She claims I helped her a lot. But still, that is not a reason to get romantically involved."

"The fact is she wants you," Travis repeated. "If you don't want her or if you have higher expectations, then don't mess up with her. There are plenty of men ready to take your place, Virgil."

"Oh, yes. Sure there are," Cory agreed. "Maggie is mighty pretty."

Virgil was frowning and he looked at Travis. "Are you talking about yourself, Travis?"

There was a second of hesitation before Travis

proclaimed emphatically, "No, of course not. I'm a gipsy, remember? A drifter with no home and with a permanent hankering to move on."

"Don't you want a home of your own Travis?" Cory asked and then blushed under the older man's scrutiny. "I mean… one day perhaps. It might be nice," he finished lamely, not knowing what caused the other's hard look.

"You might be a drifter, but there comes a time in any man's life when he knows it's time to settle down. Besides, you stayed with us since spring. Soon it will be almost a year. A record for a gipsy." Virgil drank the last of his coffee and looked in his empty mug.

"It's difficult to leave behind Miss Lottie's cooking."

Virgil laughed. "Or her mothering… Has she knitted for you one of her fuzzy colorful scarves?"

"No. She made me a vest," Travis patted his chest. "It's fuzzy and it keeps me warm. Yes, Miss Lottie is a treasure."

Cory yawned and Virgil ruffled his hair as if he

were a small boy, which inside he still was. "Time to go to bed. Cory, you take the loft, Travis and I will make do with these twin beds."

Much later, Virgil heard Travis saying, "Don't play with Maggie's heart if you're not serious, Virgil. I'm warning you."

CHAPTER 8

Overnight the wind had died down. In the morning, a thick layer of snow covered the ground, but visibility was good and there was no wind to swirl the few snowflakes that fell from the gray sky.

"Time to saddle up boys," Virgil said eager to reach the ranch house.

Finally they were ready to go. But Cory went back inside the house adding to the others' impatience. The horses were prancing and the air was cold making their breath steam.

"I wanted to leave a Thank you and Merry Christmas message to whoever is keeping this old house in top shape for lost people like us," Cory explained mounting his horse.

"That was very thoughtful of you, Cory. I'm proud of you," Virgil told him.

It was not easy riding through the freshly layered snow. It was not very deep, but it covered the ground hiding the icy spots, and often the horses slipped, so they had to keep a slow and cautious pace.

No wonder that they breathed easier, relieved, when they reached the ranch and entered the barn. The view of the barn doors decorated with lights and a wreath with a huge red bow had never been more welcome. They had just dismounted when a whirlwind entered after them.

"Virgil, how could you? You walk in here fine and dandy and it never occurred to you that I …that we have been worried. I told you I wanted to ride with you and I was right. I bet you got into trouble."

Travis raised his eyebrow and Cory opened his mouth. Then they looked at each other and started to grin.

"Virgil, if you were not in trouble yesterday, I bet you are now," Travis said smirking.

With as much dignity as he could muster, Virgil handed his bridle to Cory. "Please take care of my horse, Cory." Then he took Brianna's arm and stirred her toward the house.

There was music and voices in the kitchen and he

needed to talk to Tom about the shooter, but it could wait a few more minutes. He went into the empty family room.

"Brianna, first, you are not to talk to me like this in front of the men. You are not my employer. Tom is. And Tom treats all his men, not only me, with respect."

She bit her trembling lower lip and Virgil's eyes went there like attracted by a magnet. Darn his unruly body that still wanted her.

"I was worried. Can't you understand that?" she said looking at him with pleading eyes.

He whipped his Stetson off his head in frustration. "Frankly, no. I remember a year ago when I was thrown by a wild mustang and broke two ribs, you laughed and said a few scratches on my face won't matter because nothing could make it worse than it already is."

"Surely I didn't say that," she said horrified. Had she ever been so callous?

"I know how I look and how I am. I am not handsome and I am not good at charming the ladies with flowery words. Miss Lottie, who is an angel, explained to me, that no matter how hard we try, sometimes, there are people who don't like us. She was often in this situation growing up in foster care. These people are not going to change their opinion of us. The best we can do is to accept this, understand it's not our fault, and go on with our life." Brianna was watching him with her soft brown, doe-like eyes. To be able to continue what he wanted to say, Virgil turned to look outside at the winter white scenery. "What I'm trying to say, Brianna, is that I changed. You don't have to be afraid that I'll follow you around pestering you with my attention. I'm the first to admit I was ridiculous to persist when you made clear that you didn't want me. I moved on."

"We've all changed Virgil. I did too. Moving away from here helped me open my mind and understand better. Life, myself, what I want, everything." She raised her hand to touch him, then dropped it. She moved to stand near him at the window. "I heard you have a girlfriend…."

His face lit up with a smile. "Maggie. She's

quite… something."

"Is she beautiful?"

He hesitated trying to choose the right words to describe Maggie. "She is very pretty. She has short light-brown hair and big blue eyes. She's vibrant and lively, always smiling and animated. She reminds me of a young Goldie Hawn. Travis said that the vet's business increased since she started working there. Not that Tristan needed more business as he is swamped and his practice is booming. But the traffic increased with cowboys looking for Maggie."

"Where did you meet her? At the Maitland clinic?"

"No. I met her two years ago when I was working for Parker. She was in a difficult situation then, and I encouraged her to take her GED and move on with her life. She did well and I'm proud of her. She looked for me and you will not believe this, but she wants me," he finished, twisting his hat in his hands.

"How about you? Do you love her?"

The question gave him pause. "Well, we're just

getting to know each other. But… yeah… I like her very much. How could I not? She is lovable. I can't say I was lavished in life with love, or with people who loved me. In fact, no one ever loved me, except for my dad who died when I was six."

"What about your mother? Didn't she love you?" Brianna asked, for the first time curious to know more about him.

"Maybe she did. I don't know. She was too afraid of my stepfather, whom she married six months after Dad passed on." He sighed. "So, you see, love was in short supply for me. If Maggie offers it freely, how could I not take it and return it as well. I'd be a fool not to."

"I see…"

"And I told Tom that it is time for me to go away. He convinced me to stay until after the New Year and I promised him that I will, but after that I'll leave."

"What? Why? Is it because of me?"

"No, Brianna. I decided that before you returned to the ranch. It is time to start anew, somewhere else."

Brianna shook her head to chase away the

inexplicable feeling of sadness and emptiness his absence would leave behind. Somehow the ranch wouldn't be the same without Virgil. "I'm sorry," was all she said to atone for the moments when she'd been impatient with him in the past and for the hurtful words. And sorry for the wasted chance that they might have been friends.

Because she was close to him, she stood up on her tiptoes to kiss his cheek. Surprised, he moved his head and her lips fell squarely on his mouth. It was more than Virgil could bear. He grabbed her in his arms and deepened the kiss, just as he'd dreamed of many times.

Instead of stepping back and slapping his face silly, Brianna nestled in his arms and placed her arms around his neck. For a moment, they were lost in the unexpected passion they felt.

A wave of cold air and the loud bang of the entrance door made them jump away guiltily. Whoever entered, went into the kitchen.

Virgil raked his hair with his fingers, then picked up his hat from the floor. "I must have been insane to do that. I'm sorry. That shouldn't have happened. And you, what do you think you're doing? Are you toying with me? Is this some new game you learned in the city? I'm a man, not your plaything. At least before, you were honest in your dislike of me."

"No, it's not like that," she protested still confused by the powerful attraction she felt for him and a little scared by the contradictory feelings that assaulted her. She was not toying with him. But then why had she kissed him? How could she have been so consumed by this man's kiss? She needed to think, to clear her mind. She turned on her heel and ran to her room leaving Virgil equally confused.

Well, he had done a lot of stupid things in his life, some due to his well-known curious nature, some others just because. He had shrugged them off as a way of learning from experience. But kissing Brianna was a whopper even for him and he couldn't blame it on curiosity.

As Travis had said, he was in trouble. He had a date with Maggie, who was a wonderful person and deserved honesty. He planned to tell her the truth about his infatuation for his Boss' sister, but this kiss changed the whole confession. He couldn't in all good faith tell Maggie that his feelings for Brianna were a thing of the past.

He praised himself for being a simple man, plain and straightforward. And now he had made a mess of everything.

From the kitchen some vanilla and cinnamon aroma wafted up to his nostrils. And for once, Virgil didn't think of food. Miss Lottie, she would know what he had to do. She always had a good advice.

In the kitchen, he found Tom leaning back in a chair and admiring his wife mixing in a bowl some ingredients that smelled divinely if Virgil were tempted by cake right now and didn't have more pressing problems.

"Boss, I need to talk to you." He placed his hat on the table and took a seat. "But not yet. Now I need to talk to Miss Lottie."

Tom looked at him amused and sipped his coffee. "You know, if I were a jealous man and if I were not so full of good food, I could take exception at your wanting to have a cozy chat with my wife." He rose from the chair and chuckled at Virgil's stunned face. "Relax. It was a joke. When you're done talking to Lottie, come to my study." He refilled his coffee mug and kissing his wife, went out whistling.

"All right Virgil. What is going on?" Lottie asked placing in front of him a mug with freshly brewed hot coffee.

"I did a stupid thing, Miss Lottie. I don't know what to do," Virgil blurted out in one breath.

"Remember, as long as you are healthy, everything else can be fixed."

Virgil nodded. "Okay. I hope we can fix this. I kissed Brianna."

Lottie plopped down on another chair at the table. "What did she do? I didn't hear any yelling."

"She kissed me back. That's not the problem. I have a date with Maggie and I really wanted this dating thing to work. I like her and I feel she's good for me. I want to treat her with fairness and honesty. Brianna is only toying with me. I'm confused…"

"Virgil, first, you have to be sure of what you want. Do you want Brianna? Are your feelings for her strong and real? If the answer is yes, then you should not string Maggie along."

He looked intently into his mug. "And if they are real? She will never return my feelings. Can you see her loving me? Yes, I love her and my body craves her, but a one sided love is doomed, Miss Lottie. People like us who have been alone and unloved all our lives, we need a partner in life to respect us. Maggie likes me and wants to date me and see where this goes. I hope that maybe she is the one for me. I'm tired of loving a woman who doesn't care for me."

"I understand you perfectly well, Virgil. And what you say makes sense. Unfortunately, our heart rules our brain. You have no choice, but to be honest with Maggie. I'm sure she wants a reliable man who will return her love. She deserves to be happy."

"You're right Miss Lottie," he nodded sadly.

"…and don't forget Christmas season is a

magical one. Miracles can happen. I should know. It will happen to you too."

CHAPTER 9

Tom was in his study, sitting behind his desk looking at the monitor. "Come in Virgil. Tell me we are not short on feed. I thought we ordered plenty, but this December was one of the snowiest on record."

"No, no. We have enough till spring," Virgil said, trying not to laugh at the cute glasses perched on his Boss' nose.

"Then, I assume the feed situation is not what you want to talk about." Tom crossed his arms on top of the desk and looked at Virgil over the rim of the glasses.

"We have trouble, Boss. More accurately, I have trouble, as Travis pointed out. Someone shot at me yesterday to the east of here, right before the blizzard started."

"Are you saying we have another never-do-well holed up on a remote corner of the ranch? Just like last year when those two men had followed Lottie here and hid at the Outlaw's Rocks?"

"I don't think they are hiding there. I might be

wrong. Travis thinks I'm the target, and I'm inclined to agree because a couple of days ago, when I was in town, someone tried to run me over."

"Why didn't you tell me?"

"Because at the time I thought I was mistaken. Now I'm not so sure. Although, for the life of me I can't imagine why? I'm not rich …why?"

Tom pulled down his glasses and rubbed his eyes. "Maybe you had a fight with some cowboy recently."

"Not that I recall, and the usual disputes Saturday night at the tavern don't warrant killing a man."

"You don't know, some people are revengeful. Anyhow, you have to go to town and report it to the new sheriff. He can't do much, but it's a good idea to have it all on record."

Virgil nodded. "I was thinking that perhaps you might want me to go away for a while in order not to place the whole ranch and your family in danger." It was Christmastime and Virgil hated the idea to spend it alone, but the safety of his Boss and his family came first.

"Virgil, I told you before and I repeat that I

consider you part of this family and as such your enemy is my enemy and we have a better chance to catch him if we stay together. Just tell the sheriff the whole story. When are you going to town?"

"This afternoon. I have a date and before that I have to go again to the Cowgirl Yarn to pick up some yarn. I can fit a visit to the sheriff in between."

Tom laughed. "I didn't know you can knit. You're a man of many talents."

"Ha-ha, very funny. You know it's for Lottie."

"Yes, I do and frankly I think you're a brave man to go there not once, but twice. Those old ladies are scary. The last time Lottie dragged me there they looked at me like I was about to kidnap their darling girl, not marry her. They talked me to death."

Later that afternoon, Virgil stopped first at the sheriff's office. The old sheriff had retired last summer after asking Maitland's cook to marry him and being refused flatly. It seemed Carmelita had found the love of her life in her grandson, Little Elliott, and was not willing to be away from him, not even for her old friend, the portly sheriff. The new sheriff was young with a babyish face and glasses, and looked like a young Bill Gates. As they say, looks can be deceiving. He proved himself, when only a month into his job, he single-handedly apprehended a drug-dealing gang who terrorized ranchers south of town.

"There is not much else I can tell you, Sheriff," Virgil concluded his tale. "Except that in a blur I've seen that the truck had Montana numbers and that we found the casings and I know what type of rifle he used. That doesn't say much, as most of the men at the Maitland ranch are from Montana as is his foreman. And about the rifle, I think we all have something similar."

"Not much to go on, it's true," the young sheriff admitted. "But I agree it's too much of a coincidence and we'll keep our eyes open for any stranger in town. In summer, there are visitors aplenty, but there not so many now and a stranger will stand out. Who knows, we might get lucky and catch him."

"I just wanted you to know and to have this on

record," Virgil said, placing his Stetson on and turning to leave.

"Virgil," the sheriff called after him "No acting on your own. If you spot him, then you need to call us to deal with him. No heroic acts on your own."

Virgil nodded and left. This one sure was different from the old sheriff who preferred to wait to have the villains ready hogtied, only to collect them and cart them to jail. Of course calling the sheriff for every little disturbance was unrealistic. The ranches were sprawled over a huge area and the remote places were difficult to reach.

His next stop was at the yarn store. No one shot at him or ran him over this time and he nodded at the man in the framing store nearby, now an old acquaintance. The bell rang merrily when he entered the yarn store and the same six ladies turned to look at him.

"Ah Virgil dear, we were just talking about you," the smiling owner said.

It must have been a really uneventful week in town if he was the only subject for gossip. "I came for

Miss Lottie's yarn."

They relieved him of his coat and hat and had him ensconced in a chair. A plate with cookies and a cup of tea was placed in front of him. The cup was so delicate, ornate with pink roses and had such a tiny handle Virgil couldn't fit his index finger through it. The ladies were all looking at him expectantly. Maybe a question had been asked and he had not paid attention.

He was really inept at these social niceties. Not knowing what to do, he pinched the teacup handle with his fingers and succeeded to take a sip. He almost dropped the cup and his eyes teared up. To say the tea was spiked would have been an understatement. A very potent whiff of bourbon assaulted his nostrils.

The shop lady winked at him. "We are true cowgirls after all," she said.

Even the Santa hanging in the window seemed to be winking at him.

"This is very… warming," he said. "But I can't indulge in any more of this delicious tea. I have a date, you see."

This animated them even more and he had to tell them about Maggie.

"At the vet, you said?" one asked. "I know only Trish, a very nice girl. She always takes care of my Horace. He's bound to pee there because he is afraid of needles. And I don't blame him."

"It can't be Trish because she's married. I don't know any Maggie. Does she knit?"

"Ah...I don't know. I'm sure she does," Virgil said trying to extricate himself from the chair.

"Wait," another said, producing a small comb and attempting to style his hair. He could have told her that after placing the Stetson on, all the styling would become nonexistent. "Too bad. I wanted to introduce you to my sister's cousin-in-law, a very nice girl."

The shop owner came with a skein of very soft rainbow colored wool. "Do you think this is what Lottie had in mind? She said to be colorful, for a vest for her husband."

Virgil thought of Tom riding his stallion in this pink, fuchsia, and purple vest and grinned. Eh no, he couldn't do it. "Maybe more like this earthy tone," he said, picking up a nice brownish skein.

"Tobacco, yes, you have a good eye." The lady smiled approvingly, packing the brown wool.

Tom, you owe me – Virgil thought.

When he was ready to go, the hairstylist told him, "Please bring your Maggie here. We'd love to meet her." And when he looked at her he was surprised to see that she meant it. It was not just a polite invitation.

"You know, I think I will, because I'm sure Maggie would be delighted to meet you all, too." He nodded and left with a spring in his step. Strange, but somehow he did not dread meeting Maggie and telling her his confession. He knew Maggie would understand.

Maggie lived with an older woman and her niece in a small house close to the veterinarian clinic. She came flying down the porch to meet Virgil. She had a nice denim skirt on and booties with high heels.

"Lord, Maggie your legs will freeze without jeans," he said the first thing that crossed his mind.

She looked at him crestfallen. "I wanted to look nice. It's my first real date."

Virgil cursed himself for being an insensitive clod. He cupped her cheek in his palm. "You look splendid. You are beautiful, Maggie. Don't you know that? You could dress in pajamas and be beautiful, because your beauty comes from inside you."

He kissed briefly her soft, trembling lips. It was nice, in a comforting way. Again no bells and whistles, the earth didn't shatter.

"I know a little taqueria that has delicious Mexican food. Would you like to go there?" Maggie asked when they were in his truck.

"No, Mags. As I told you before, this is my first official date too. Single women met in taverns don't count as dates. I'm glad you're so beautifully dressed. We are going to The Cavalryman Steakhouse restaurant."

"Virgil, that is one of the most expensive restaurants in Laramie. They have fabric tablecloths," Maggie said.

"Yep. I already made reservations there."

The restaurant was located on the grounds of the old Fort Sanders, in an old building, updated several times and still keeping the historical character and its rich tradition. The tables were covered with white tablecloths and the walls had framed historical photographs from times long gone.

As they were led to their table, Virgil looked at Maggie, clutching his hand a little intimidated and yet her eyes were sparkling while admiring the rooms decorated like in the old time. She was so pretty in her skirt and booties, and his heart constricted with emotion. He felt a deep affection for this brave girl facing the world alone like him, and profound regret that what he felt for her was more brotherly than passionate.

He ordered the Bison Ribeye Steak, sourced locally from Wyoming ranches, and Maggie chose the Country Fried Steak.

There was nice country music playing in the background. At least they could enjoy a nice evening and tomorrow would take care of itself.

CHAPTER 10

They finished the scrumptious dessert, a western bread pudding, and were lingering over coffee. Virgil knew it was time for him to talk.

"Two years ago, I was working at the Parker ranch and I liked to explore the more remote corners of the land. I was riding to an interesting-looking butte when I saw at a distance a rider. He scrutinized me for a moment, then raising his chin in an unmistakable challenge he spurred his horse in a race toward the butte. I followed him and as my stallion was much more powerful than the workhorse he was riding I was sure I'd overtake him, no matter how skilled a rider he was. I'd have won that race if a gust of wind didn't take his hat off and a long mane of dark hair flowed down her back. I was so surprised that she was a woman that I stopped urging on my horse. Needless to say, she reached the butte first, turned to look at me with disappointment and said, "You're not much of a rider, are you?" Then she left me there looking after her, as she galloped away with skill and elegance."

"You shouldn't have let her win the race,"
Maggie said, a competitive gleam in her eyes.

Virgil agreed. "In retrospect, I know it was a
mistake. At the time, I was not only surprised she was a
woman, but I acted from an instinctive chivalry, and
stopped my horse, letting her win. And to be perfectly
honest, I fell in love with her instantly."

"Just like that, hmm? And then?"

"I didn't know who she was and I didn't see her
for a while. Parker retired and let his son-in-law, Raul
Maitland, manage the ranch. He brought some cowboys
from Montana including a new foreman to replace
Gimpy Fred. Not bad guys, but they tended to gang
together. I was the odd man out. I decided to move on.
After I saw Brianna again at a social gathering, it so
happened that Tom Gorman was looking to hire new men
and I thought to move to his ranch to be closer to her."

"Oh, Virgil."

"I know. That was the second mistake. I started
following her around, trying to be nice and helpful."

A VISITOR FOR CHRISTMAS

Maggie caught his hand between her two smaller ones over the table. "Let me guess, she didn't return your feelings."

"No. In fact, she was annoyed by my open admiration." Virgil took a deep breath. "I know I'm not handsome, but her disdain made me feel ugly and stupid."

"What? No, Virgil. You are strong and good, trustful, and you project confidence." She clutched his hand tighter. "Men don't need to be pretty to be attractive."

"Last year, after Christmas she ran away with a drifter who worked over winter at the Maitland ranch. I waited and waited for her to come back. I even thought perhaps it was a good thing. She'd see that not every handsome man is worth running away with."

"Did she come back?"

"When I met you at the vet and when I agreed that we should date, she had not and I had decided to move on with my life, go to other places. And I meant it." He looked into his empty cup and signaled the server to refill it. "She came back last week. She was perfectly composed like she'd left yesterday for a visit to town."

"What did Gorman say?"

"She's his sister. He was happy to have her back."

"How did her adventure end?"

"Not as bad as we'd all feared. Tom kept tabs on her. She lived in Denver and had parted ways with the drifter a long time ago. He left as soon as he found out she didn't own any part of the family ranch."

Maggie looked at him. The sparkle in her eyes was gone. She was bracing for what she perceived was bad news to come. "So how do you fell about her coming back?" she asked in a small voice.

"At first, I thought nothing had changed for me. I'll leave soon after the New Year. But she seems to have changed, or so she claims. I told her I'm dating a wonderful girl, but then she kissed me, which confused me entirely."

"I see," Maggie repeated.

"Look, I want to be completely honest with you.

The truth is that Brianna's return only precipitated what
we would have realized sooner or later. I like you very
much, Maggie. I have a lot of affection for you. I think
you are a one in a million girl, but I don't think we have
the kind of chemistry that sparks passion. I would fight
all the bad men in the world and face scary nightmares
for you, but I don't know if I could kiss you passionately.
Sometimes I'm mad with myself, because you are the
perfect woman for me. I've been alone all my life and
I'm starved for someone to love me truly. But you
deserve more. We deserve true love."

"How do we know if we'll ever find it?"

"We can hope. Miss Lottie said that
Christmastime is a magic season and miracles happen."

"Do you believe in miracles, Virgil?"

"I never had any miracles in my life, but what is a
man to do without hope?"

Maggie looked at him weighing what he said.
"You know, I worked really hard to study and overcome
all my deficiencies and to get my GED. I started taking
some college classes and I know I can get my associate

degree in a few years. But I discovered recently that I'm lonely. I don't have many friends. Trish, the vet assistant is nice, but she's married with children and her life struggles are very different than mine. I thought of you because you were the only one who encouraged me in a very difficult time and because I knew you were alone too. I need a friend, Virgil. Do you want to be my friend, to be the one I call after work to complain about the mess I had to clean in a stall left by Mr. Both's cow and the scratch I got from Miss Mary's cat? Can I talk to you about how difficult I find some chemistry problems? You don't need to kiss me Virgil, but could we go to eat together once in a while at a much less expensive restaurant or to dance at the Cowboy Saloon together?"

He smiled at her. "I would like that very much, Maggie. I've never had any real friends in my life and I'd like that. But what about all the cowboys who assault Tristan's clinic every day hoping to see you?"

Maggie frowned. "What cowboys?"

"Travis told me that the traffic to the clinic increased tenfold since you started working there, and many unattached men are trying to get your attention. You are young, Maggie. You should date men you might like, give yourself a chance to find 'the one' for you."

"I'm not going to find my 'one and only' among those cowboys. And who is this Travis who knows my business and talks about me?"

"Travis is a good man. Keeps to himself, but so do most of us. He's a rodeo champion."

"Ah, now I know him. He's the 'love them and leave them' kind of man. Very handsome and vain, a show off. I doubt he won any competitions. It's all talk."

Virgil blinked. Women had such a different perception about things than men. "Travis handsome and vain?" Granted Virgil was not exactly an expert in what women wanted, but still…"Travis is a shorter guy, around thirty, thirty-five years old, and he won a lot of rodeo competitions, some at high level. I don't know if he ever won the All Around title at the Nationals, but he has a bunch of champion belt buckles. And he is not vain. There is not much privacy in the bunkhouse and we saw his trophies and asked. Cory especially wanted to know. Otherwise, he wouldn't have talked about himself being a champ."

"He's not any shorter than others, even if he looks short compared to you. And he is handsome in a dark, brooding way. Like a western Heathcliff," she said sighing.

"Who's this Heath fellow?"

"A character in a classic novel… So you think Travis was a real rodeo champion?"

"I know he was. I don't know details because as I said, like all of us, he keeps his cards close to his chest. But he is a good man. He saved my life during the blizzard. And in general, when work needs to be done, he just does it, without complaining. I like him."

"If he saved your life, I guess… I like him too."

The server came near their table. "Well folks, do you need anything else? More coffee?"

It was almost closing time and Virgil paid the bill and they went outside. It was not snowing, but it was very cold.

In short time, the powerful engine of the truck

started to blast warm air through the vents. "Are you warmer Maggie?" Virgil asked while driving through the almost deserted streets of Laramie.

"Now I am," she laughed. "I enjoyed myself and the food was fabulous, but can I invite you to the Cowboy Saloon Saturday night. They have live music and dancing. Would you come with me, Virgil?"

"I would love to."

When they stopped in front of Maggie's house, she turned to him and cupping his face in her hand she kissed him on the cheek. "You're a good man, Virgil. Thank you for being my friend." Then she was out of his truck and running to the door without waiting for him to accompany her.

Virgil looked after her, looked at the small house, the only one without decorations on the street. Only in a window upstairs there was a silver star and a string of lights around it. He would bet it was Maggie's window. He made a promise to bring her to the ranch and enjoy a real Christmas celebration with the Gormans. Maggie deserved it.

He started the engine and drove back to the ranch. He was deep in thought, but outside of town the roads, although ploughed, were slippery. There were patches of ice and the truck fishtailed from time to time requiring his full attention.

His radio played Christmas music and he was still thinking of Maggie, when suddenly he saw a dark shape in the middle of the road. It looked like an abandoned vehicle. This was the secondary road that farther split, to the left to the Gorman's Diamond G ranch, to the right to the extensive Maitland ranch and at the end Parker's spread.

Which one of the cowboys working at either one of the ranches could be so irresponsible, even drunk to leave a truck with the lights off at night in the middle of the road?

Virgil stopped his truck behind it and went there to investigate. It looked abandoned. Maybe the driver had run out of gas. He approached the driver's side and looked inside. He heard a noise behind him and tried to turn around. Too late. A heavy object hit his head and the world turned black.

CHAPTER 11

"Virgil, wake up! Virge!" Someone was slapping his face and he batted away ineffectively at the hand. His head felt like it was splintering into a million pieces. He opened one eye. He lay sprawled in the middle of the icy road. The light from the two headlights of a truck was the only light in the otherwise dark night and it hurt his eyes.

"Virgil, I need you to wake up and get up. I'll help you climb into my truck, but I can't carry you." Travis was looking at him with worry. At least he had stopped slapping his face.

"I thought you bull riders were the strongest guys in the rodeo," Virgil muttered attempting to sit up and a sudden wave of dizziness made him grab Travis's coat to steady himself.

"Of course, we are strong, but we ride the bulls, not lift them up." He pulled Virgil up and supported him as he was a little wobbly. "Do you see one or two of me?" he asked.

"You're a good guy Travis, but two of you would

be too much. Someone hit my head. There was this dark truck stopped in the middle of the road with the lights off and when I looked inside someone came from behind and hit me," Virgil said, climbing in Travis' truck. "Wait. What about my truck? Maybe I could drive. I don't think I lost consciousness completely. I have a hard head. I think I was only dazed by the hit."

"I'll come later with Cory to drive your truck back to the ranch. Right now you have a goose egg at the back of your head and you need to be taken care of. You'd be surprised what a good nurse Tiny Pete is."

"Angel is too. He can minister wounds and sprains well... Did you see anything?"

"The guy who hit you was shorter than you, had a shovel, and was raising it to bash your head again when I stopped right there. First, I honked the horn louder to scare him, then I grabbed my rifle from the back and got out. He threw the shovel on the side of the road and climbed in his truck and gunned the engine. He drove to town, not to one of the ranches. Was it a robbery in progress? Was he a real enemy who wanted you dead?

But why hit you instead of shooting you like he did before, if it was the same man?"

These questions made Virgil's headache intensify. He had no idea he was so important that someone would want him dead. But coincidences added up and he couldn't ignore them.

Tiny Pete not only placed a plaster on his wound to reduce the swelling, but forced him to do some silly motions that made the others laugh, like to touch his nose and look at his finger. Tiny Pete claimed that that's what a doctor asked him to do after he hit his head jumping over the fence, running from an enraged bull.

Later, Virgil lay on his bunk bed. Although he was tired, he could not sleep. He looked through the tiny window at the dark night outside thinking of the recent events. Usually he did that at the end of the day planning the next day's work. But now he was unsettled and unable to relax and sleep. He heard Travis turning in the bed above him.

"Yo, Travis," he whispered.

"Hmm, what?"

"I wanted to say thank you. You saved my life twice."

"Hmm," Travis muttered something unintelligible.

"I owe you. I don't like to be in debt, but there you have it, I owe you."

"Go to sleep, Virgil. You don't owe me anything. I did what you would have done in my place. I'm no hero, trust me."

What a strange thing to say – Virgil thought. Usually, he'd let it go. A man is entitled to his privacy and his secrets. But he was in a strange mood tonight, questioning his decisions and the way his life had turned out.

"Travis, do you ever think of settling down?"

"Remember that Cory asked me the same question. I'm a gipsy at heart. I can't settle down."

"You could if you wanted. I mean, you achieved something important, won trophies, proved you're good."

"I had a dream, Virgil and I didn't achieve it. So, the way I see it, I failed." Travis turned again in his

115

narrow bed, his sleep now gone. "How was your date today? Is this what all this talk is about? You want to get hitched and are not sure it will work."

"Partly. It made me think about what is important to me."

"I sure hope Maggie is. I told you not to fool around if you are not serious about her."

"Maggie and I, we have an understanding."

That got Travis's attention. "Did you propose to her? Are you two engaged already?"

"Engaged? No, of course not. Maggie and I are friends."

"Maggie loves you, Virgil. You are the only man she agreed to date. And trust me, there are scores of cowboys who asked her out, including me."

That gave Virgil pause. "You asked her out?"

"Shh, not so loud. You'll awake the others."

"Not a chance. Tiny Pete is snoring and Cory is deeply asleep, out like a light. Angel is in the barn."

"What's he doing in the barn?"

Familiar with the mountain man's odd habits,

Virgil shrugged. "Finding peace."

"Ah, okay then. I asked Maggie out three times. The first time was more like, 'there is a movie at the theater, how about coming with me'. Not a wise way to put it into words. It sounded like I didn't care if she came or not."

"What did she say?"

"She said, 'not in your dreams' or something like that. I waited two more weeks before I asked her out again. This time to a country music concert and I was very polite. I said I would enjoy her company. She answered that she was busy. I don't know why I'm telling you all this. It's personal stuff."

Virgil smiled. "You're telling me this because I might have a concussion and you hope by tomorrow I'll forget everything. Humor me and tell me about the third."

"I don't think I'd have asked her out a third time if I didn't hear her talking to Trish that she loves to dance and she'd like to go to the Cowboy Saloon on Saturday because there was a live band. Of course, Trish, married with three kids and a husband, has no time to go to dances. So I told her that I liked her very much and it would be my pleasure to take her out to dance."

"And what did she say?"

"She hesitated only because of her desire to go dancing, not because she considered giving me a chance. She said, "No, thank you. Phony rodeo champions don't interest me". Why phony? And I never told her I was a champion… But anyhow, I gave up. Maybe it's better this way. I'm a gipsy, never in one place and she has her own plans for life. That's why I think she loves you. You are the only one she agreed to date."

"Not exactly. When I met her two years ago, she had no one. Her stepbrother almost got her involved in a messy and illegal situation, robbery, kidnapping, extortion. He's in jail. Parker and I decided she was an innocent caught in the middle of this. She had protected Parker's grandson and facilitated his escape from the bad guys. I encouraged her to get her GED and make a life for herself. I'm one of the very few men she trusts if not the only one. Life taught her to be cautious and wary of men. She knows me."

Travis turned again in the upper bed. "Maybe. But she likes you. She certainly doesn't like me."

"Hmm, not true. I remember distinctly that she said you are handsome. And that surprised me, but what do I know about men's looks?"

"She said that?"

"Yep. And I mentioned that you are short, but she seemed unfazed, arguing that any man would look short compared to me. Who can understand women and what they like in a man?" Virgil said genuinely puzzled.

"Now, see here, I'm not short," Travis protested. "I'm the right height for bull riding."

"True. If that was what you were doing all your life. Now, I have an idea. Why don't you come this Saturday to the Cowboy Saloon?"

"Why?"

"To dance of course. And surprise! I'll be there too."

"You want me to dance with you? I think your concussion is making you confused."

"Not to dance with me. I'll be there with Maggie."

Pause. "Hmm, not a good idea, Virgil."

"What have you got to lose? Be prepared to be rejected a forth time. Or who knows? Women are unpredictable. One day they curse you and call you ugly, the next, they kiss you senseless."

Travis chuckled. "Did that happen to you recently?"

Virgil squirmed in his bed and tried to evade answering. "I was talking in general."

"In general, I think you aim too high. Not because you're not good enough for our Boss' sister, but because she is too haughty. If you add to this the fact that she has some money from her father... Of course, I don't know her well. She just returned home. I might be wrong."

"Do you think I don't know?" Virgil asked bitterly. "I know that I'm a penniless cowboy without charm or good looks. I loved her from the first moment I saw her. I knew she was the one for me."

"Too bad she didn't know this also."

Virgil continued his line of thought. "After she left, at first I was hurting so much I thought I was not going to survive. Then the work helped me and I convinced myself that if I move on and I don't live here, where everything reminds me of her, I could go on with my life. Then she came back and turned me into a smitten idiot once again."

"Virgil, my man, you've got it bad," Travis observed without adding that he couldn't see a happy ending for his friend.

"I'm hopeless. You saw how she tore into me when we came back from Maitland's homestead yesterday."

"Hmm…That is not necessarily a bad thing. She was worried about you. It could be that she does care about you a little."

Tiny Pete gave a mighty snore and sat up startled on his bed. "Will you two gossipy people stop clucking in the middle of the night? What is so fiery dang important that it can't wait until tomorrow?"

CHAPTER 12

Brianna had a purpose this morning. Steering clear of the kitchen and the temptation of all sorts of good food Lottie was cooking, she stopped in the family room to turn on the lights on the tall Christmas tree, and looked at the funny drawing of a puppy made by the youngest boy, Billy. The boys' paternal grandfather, Sam W Donovan was to arrive from Texas for the Christmas celebration any day now. Somewhere in the house Christmas music was playing and the house smelled of pine mixed with vanilla and spices or whatever was cooking in the kitchen. A fire burned in the fireplace, crackling merrily from time to time.

It was good to be home and she loved spending Christmas with her family. In the short time, less than a year, since her sister-in-law, Lottie had been married with Tom, she had achieved a miracle. This was truly a home and Brianna was happy to be back. She had hidden gifts for everyone in her closet, including the ranch hands, all carefully wrapped, adorned with colorful bows.

She looked outside to see if it snowed again. Her eyes were immediately attracted by a tall, powerful man, without a winter coat despite the cold, wearing only a plaid shirt and a blue vest, probably knitted by Lottie. His muscles were strained by the effort to raise bales of hay in the wagon. When did plain Virgil turn into such a fine figure of a man? And what was this nonsense about him having a girlfriend? Although, if Brianna liked how he looked, was it impossible that some other girl might admire him or be attracted to him? He certainly knew how to kiss a girl until her knees turned to jelly.

Brianna twirled on her heel and humming along with the music, marched into her brother's study.

Tom was behind his desk frowning at what he was reading on his monitor. He had wire rimmed glasses perched on his nose and he looked so domesticated that Brianna wondered if he hadn't developed a small paunch with all the good life that Lottie had brought to this family.

"Ah Brianna. How are you? This weather is

driving me crazy, keeping me holed up here instead of riding outside on the range. We didn't have that much snow in December since the winter I was twelve and the snow reached up to the windows."

"I think the men are going to spread some more hay for the stranded cattle. They should hurry as another snowfall is imminent before dark," she said taking a seat in the old leather chair where she used to climb when she was a little girl to see if Daddy had some peppermints. He rarely did and in time he became more and more distracted. After their mother's death, his heart was not much into anything. He smoked his lungs to death like he didn't care. And he probably didn't. The ranch situation had been dire when he passed away and Tom took over. Tom made tremendous efforts to make it prosperous again. "You worked very hard over the years, Tom. You can take it easier from time to time now."

Tom looked at her surprised. He'd never heard his sister praise him. Maybe she didn't know either that he appreciated her work on the ranch over the years. He crossed his arms over his chest. "What is it, Brie? I'm glad you came back home. I have always considered that without your work and Chris', I don't think I'd have succeeded to rebuild the ranch the way it is now, one to be proud of. So tell me, is this about your inheritance? I never meant to deprive you of it. It's yours...."

Brianna took a deep breath. "Yes. This is about my inheritance. And about my plans. Do you know that after you refused to release my money I was so upset that Dad didn't want me to have any part of the ranch, and you didn't want me to have my money, that I decided by all means, I'll give it up, I don't need it."

"Brie, this is your inheritance. Father wanted to protect you against dishonest men because you were easily charmed by their lies. He worked a lifetime to save all that money. That's why he left me in charge. But the money is yours. I can't touch it or use it for any purpose."

"Then why did you refuse to release it to me?"

"Because you ran away with an untrustworthy man..."

"I did not run away with Joe. I was not a

teenager. I left with him because he was amusing and at the time it suited me. Tom, I was almost thirty years old. I was an adult. You should have trusted me."

"No, Brianna, you didn't just leave. Lottie told me that you needed to be free and to know more of the world and I tried to understand. But you didn't leave saying goodbye and keeping in touch. You ran away like a teenager, leaving behind a short message. This hurt us all, me, Chris, although he didn't complain, the kids, Billy and Wyatt, who didn't understand why their favorite new aunt vanished. Lottie thought it was somehow because of her that you left. And Virgil was hurt because he adored you and his world changed without you. Between us, for him it was for the best to be rid of his childish infatuation and to mature into the responsible man he is now."

"I'm sorry, Tom." Brianna bent her head down and her voice trembled. "I understand I hurt you all and I'm very sorry. I never intended it and frankly I didn't think you will care so much. You see, for years I had these contradictory feelings. I loved the ranch and riding on our land, but there was also a pent-up frustration in me, a dissatisfaction ever since I knew Dad didn't appreciate me enough to leave me a part of the land. And it grew. A person needs to have his or her place to call his own. I didn't have one."

"Father didn't want to split the ranch and I agree with him. This is your home, you were born here and I thought you considered it yours too."

Brianna looked at him with moist eyes. "No dear. It's not the same and it's not mine."

"I'm sorry you feel this way. I know I'm the owner of the ranch on paper, but I see myself more like a steward, taking care of it for all our family."

"And you did a fine job, considering in what condition the ranch was when Dad passed away. But each person has dreams of his own. Let me tell you what my dreams are. This year in Denver I learned a lot of things about myself. I lived in a minuscule studio apartment in a nice young neighborhood, in Stapleton. Although it was small, it was my place, and I loved it. I picked cheap pieces of furniture that fit just right, pillows, colorful rugs and decorated it with prints and flowers."

Tom smiled at her. It'd been a long time since he'd seen his sister so enthusiastic. "How about working in a restaurant? TJ Lomax kept tabs on you and he informed me that you were well."

A contrite smile was his answer. "I was afraid that if I kept in touch with you, you'd come flying to my rescue. I didn't want that. I needed to prove to myself that I could survive on my own. And I did. I was hired as server, and promoted to hostess. Until one day the manager had a family emergency, some others called in sick, and the chef was pulling his hair out for not having the right ingredients for the day's special. It was chaos and no one to take control. Then I stepped in and discovered that every crisis situation can be fixed by staying calm and improvising. The next day I was promoted assistant manager."

"Good for you. TJ didn't tell me this."

"I had a good life there, nice friends and neighbors and I loved to go hiking on the numerous trails, to browse the stores, libraries, go to the theatre. It was fun."

"How did you decide to come back?"

"The day after Thanksgiving I was walking and looking at the stores putting up Christmas decorations and playing Christmas music inside and I remembered the last Christmas at home and felt so homesick that I knew it was time to return."

"We are all so happy that you're back, Brie. Now tell me about your plans."

"Well, I changed my mind about the money. If Dad wanted me to have it, then I'll take it and put it to good use."

"I already told the estate attorney to release the funds to you unconditionally anytime you want."

Brianna nodded. "I appreciate this," She paused thinking how to explain better to her brother her unusual ideas. "I want to buy a place of my own. I'm aware that my inheritance is not enough to buy a big ranch. A small one would be good enough for what I plan to do."

"I could give you some money to supplement

what you need for a decent size ranch, not as big as this one of course, but with luck we might find a nice piece of land. I can't give you a part of this ranch, as Dad specifically mentioned in his will the ranch is not to be divided or sold."

"Thank you for your offer, Tom, but the inheritance will be sufficient. I need a smaller place because I want to raise goats," she looked at him anxiously trying to gauge his reaction.

To give him his due, Tom didn't blow up at this news. Calmly, he took off his glasses and after counting to ten in silence, he asked, "Why goats? I mean we have a few, mostly for the kids' amusement. Tristan saddled me with one and she started multiplying in no time at all."

"Funny… However, I am serious. Working in the restaurant industry made me aware about the new trends. As you know people are more inclined toward healthy food and organic produce. Goat cheese is the type most often used in restaurants and in demand in deli stores. Sandwiches, salads, appetizers, even entrees use mostly goat cheese than any other kind, because of the low fat content and pleasant taste."

Tom raked his hair with his fingers. When he thought life was becoming easier, it threw him another challenge, another mountain to climb. What could he do? A promise was a promise. "I'll help you the best I can. I can't say I know much about goats, not to mention making cheese from their milk. Ugh! The goats sort of... get into everyone's way in the barn and around it. The boys play with them... Now, if you want to start with a few heads of cattle, then I could help you more. Both with knowledge and material."

Brianna laughed at him. Frankly she'd expected an even more deterrent reaction from Tom at her outlandish ideas. Tom was a rather stodgy rancher. He didn't like to be taken out of the familiar pattern of the life and work he knew. "No. No cattle. Only goats. And it's going to be my enterprise. Mine alone, win or fail. Not that I don't appreciate your offer to help. I do."

Tom shuddered. What could he say? "All right. Goats it is."

CHAPTER 13

It was Saturday night and despite the chilly air the ranch hands decided to go to the dance hall.

"Who said a bunkhouse doesn't smell nice?" Tiny Pete said looking in the mirror and twirling his moustache.

"No one would dare. It reeks of cologne in here," Travis commented, sitting on the bed and wondering which boots to wear. The new ones looked great, but they were not yet worn in and they pinched his toes. The old ones were more comfortable, but they looked a bit scuffed. With so many people dancing, no one would see his boots. However, he decided that for this occasion and the chance that a pretty blue-eyed girl might agree to dance with him, he could wear the new ones and endure a little toe-pinching for one night.

"I was the one invited to the dance. How come all of you are going too?" Virgil muttered his protest, attempting again to comb his hair with a side part, although it didn't matter because the Stetson covered his hairdo. His blue denim shirt was clean and new and he looked pretty spiffy.

"We're not going with you; we're going on our own. We have to watch over that little gal of yours, just in case a rowdy cowboy wants to cut in or becomes inebriated and aggressive," Tiny Pete clarified still looking in his mirror.

"I can take care of her," Virgil replied.

Angel had been the only one who didn't want to go, but had been out vetoed. They found a nice, ironed red shirt and an assorted sweater and now he waited by the door, his arms crossed over his chest, with such a dark look that no girl would be so brave as to invite him to the dance floor.

"You young man, stay with us and lay off the alcohol even if you are of age," Tiny Pete counseled Cory.

Travis patted Cory on the back. "What's the point of going to the Cowboy Saloon if not to drink and dance? It would be no fun to sit with the old men on the side of the room."

Meanwhile, in the family room of the ranch house, Brianna and Lottie's little boys were playing Lego on the floor in front of the majestic Christmas tree.

"The firetruck goes woom, woom," Billy said pushing the firetruck in front of the newly built fire station.

Lottie came in. "Tell me when you want to have dinner. The men are not dinning with us tonight."

"Why not?" Brianna asked.

"It's Saturday night. They are going out."

"To the tavern to shoot pool and get drunk?"

"Not this time," Lottie corrected her taking a seat near Tom on the couch. "They are going to the Cowboy Saloon to dance."

"To the Cowboy Saloon… hmm… Chris," Brianna grabbed her brother's arm to get his attention. "Let's go too. It's Saturday night. Let's go dance."

"Are you daft? I can't hear the music and even if I did hear it, I don't know to dance."

"Who cares. There will be so much noise that

you'll be lucky not to hear. As for in-line dancing, that's easy. Just do what the others do."

"A deaf person can't dance," he answered trying to go back to what he was reading on his laptop.

"Chris," Brianna shook his arm again. "This is your excuse not to go. It will work out, you'll see. Now let's go."

And so Brianna bulldozed him and the two of them arrived at the Cowboy Saloon shortly after the others. The dancing hall was full and Brianna had been right, the live band was quite loud, the singer was giving his all, clenching the microphone to be heard above the raucous talk of the people crowded around the bar and moving on the dance floor.

Maggie was waiting for Virgil in front of her house and this time he remembered to compliment her on her looks. She was really pretty in a black skirt and a fuzzy blue sweater under the winter jacket. She had the same short booties on. "I'll have to fight men off, left and right, when they'll see you, Mags. You are very pretty."

It was the right thing to say, and she blushed a little embarrassed.

When they entered the dancing hall, Virgil wrinkled his nose. The crowded room and the loud music combined with the noisy people were not to his taste. He wondered how these cowboys, who lived in open spaces and breathed fresh air every day, could enjoy rubbing against each other in this overcrowded room. But then Maggie turned to him, happy, her eyes sparkling with excitement and he forgot his thoughts. He was here to make her happy and to see that she had fun.

Virgil placed a hand at her waist so none of the single cowboys would get any ideas. To his surprise, Virgil saw Tiny Pete on the dance floor holding close a woman twice as wide as he was and swinging slowly around in total disregard of the alert rhythm of the music performed by the band.

Travis was sitting at the bar, brooding, with a beer mug frothing in front of him.

"Do you want to have a beer at the bar or go dance?" Virgil asked looking at the crowded dance floor.

A VISITOR FOR CHRISTMAS

Maggie's attention was on the stage. "Look, Hugh McCaffrey is going to sing. I'm so happy to hear and see him in person. Come," she said and pulled him by the hand to the front of the stage.

Virgil had no idea who this Hugh person was, but he followed Maggie. Hugh was a cowboy 'past his prime', playing to his audience, especially the women. Virgil could swear Hughie had never worked cattle in his life. But he sung a sentimental ballad about a cowboy abandoned at the side of the highway by his lover and the women were all in tears including Maggie.

Travis tapped him on the shoulder. "I'm cutting in."

Virgil rolled his eyes. So much for teaching him to be charming. "We are not dancing. You can't cut in," Virgil told him.

Travis was stubborn. "I'm cutting in whatever you are doing." He grabbed Maggie's hand.

"Travis, it doesn't work like that." Virgil tried to temper him down. What had gotten into him?

Maggie touched his arm. "Virgil, it's okay. I can

dance this one with him."

"Maggie, I promised you a good time. You don't have to." But Travis dragged Maggie to the middle of the floor. Virgil had to keep an eye on them. He'd never seen Travis inebriated, but if he was now, Virgil had to protect Maggie. Darn Travis, what kind of a courting was this? He looked more like a caveman with such manners.

Tiny Pete waltzed nearby with the same mature woman in his arms and passing by Virgil, he winked. At the bar, Cory was listening to an older man, another one of the cowboys perpetually following the rodeo competitions. Angel was nowhere to be seen. He may have gone outside to find peace.

Virgil looked around the room and his jaw dropped when he saw Brianna dancing, throwing her arms and her body in all directions to the fast rhythm of the music. In front of her, Chris was swaying, shuffling his feet, trying to follow her. What was she doing here in a bar for rowdy cowboys and dragging her brother with her?

The music ended in a tremendous noise of drums

and yells and the dancers applauded enthusiastically. Virgil turned to see what Maggie was doing, but his attention was distracted by what the man on the stage was saying.

"And now folks, to allow Hugh to catch his breath, we invite one of you local talents to sing on the stage with us." He looked around the room. "Who wants to sing with us? What, no one? What about you cowboy?" He looked at Chris who was closer to the stage and was looking straight at him to be able to read his lips. "Come up here and we'll help you." He extended his hand to Chris and lifted him onto the stage. Once up there, Chris took the guitar abandoned on the chair. He didn't pay any attention to the other man.

"So what are you going to sing? Tell us and we'll sing along."

Brianna opened her mouth to tell him that Chris can't hear, when someone in the hall shouted, "Let him sing, boys."

Chris adjusted the microphone, touched the guitar cords lightly and started to sing an old song by Garth

Brooks. It was hauntingly beautiful and sad about unfulfilled love without hope. The noise in the hall trickled down until it stopped entirely. When Chris finished, people clapped their hands, whistled, and asked for more, but he didn't hear them. Opening his eyes slowly, he set down the guitar and jumped down from the stage.

Afraid this unknown cowboy might steal their glory, the band hastened to play their music and the famous Hugh McCaffrey returned to the microphone. The dancing continued.

Only Brianna understood what Chris was feeling. "Chris you were great. I had no idea you can sing like that." She embraced her brother.

"Could," he corrected her. "I could sing. As time goes by, the sounds I make will lose quality because I can't hear them."

"I'm sorry," she said realizing what a loss he experienced.

He touched her cheek gently. "It's all right, Brie. I came to terms with my disability and I accepted that in time my voice will deteriorate almost completely." He looked at her sadly. "Can we go home now?"

Virgil intervened. "I'll take her home, Chris, don't worry. You can go."

"What about your girlfriend, Virgil?" Brianna asked, looking after her departing brother.

Virgil looked at the dancing couples and saw Maggie swaying slowly with her head on Travis's shoulder. "Let me talk to Travis." He mingled among the dancing couples until he reached Maggie and Travis.

Travis looked at him and mouthed, "Go away."

"Virgil, do you mind if Travis takes me home?" Maggie asked him, looking at him with her wonderful, innocent blue eyes.

Virgil hesitated. Maggie was his responsibility today. "Look, something came up. I'll let you take Maggie home, but take good care of her. She's very precious to me. Do we understand each other, Travis?"

The other man nodded curtly.

CHAPTER 14

Virgil turned around, but Brianna was not behind him. He found her near the bar with three cowboys waving tanks with beer while telling her a story. Great. Now, he had to confront three drunk cowboys.

When they saw him they looked him up and down to asses their chances. He was taller and more muscular than either one of them and unless they fought dirty, he could dispatch all three in no time at all.

Brianna smiled and climbed down from the bar stool. "Tim here was telling me how they do the steer wrestling in rodeo. Let's dance, Virgil."

"And you certainly don't know how and needed a lecture on the subject of steer wrestling. Brianna, you could give Tim lessons." It was a very fast paced dance and there was no more talking.

"Oh, this was fun," she said when the song ended. The next one was a slow moving one and Brianna pulled him closer and put her hands around his neck.

How strange, Brianna thought. A memory came

to her mind, from a long time ago, ten years or so. She had been invited to prom by a very handsome boy. He was not her boyfriend, but he had just broken up with his girlfriend and to spite her, he had invited Brianna to the prom. She chose a pretty dress and looked great. She had so much hope and dreamed of how he would fall in love with her – dreams of a naïve young girl.

What happened next had come as a surprise to her. When her handsome prince took her in his arms for a slow dance, her first instinct was to step back. The nearness of him was repulsive. His cologne was a bit strong, but in all fairness he did not smell bad. To this day she couldn't understand why she disliked his touch. The closer to him he pulled her, the more claustrophobic she felt. Wrong chemistry, or lack of it... She had felt the need to run for the hills.

In the end, she suppressed the need to push him away and smiled prettily although not very encouraging. He drove her home and said good-night without the traditional kiss and without promises of another date. The next day, his girlfriend told Brianna smugly that she and the boy had patched things up. Brianna smiled and sincerely wished them happiness.

It was strange that just the opposite happened with Virgil. When she had first seen him, she had thought he was ugly and clownish. Not to mention that he tended to stutter and be clumsy in her presence. His open admiration was not at all flattering, but mostly annoying. After a year of absence, she found him to be a different man. Without her around, he had matured into a confident man, respected by the others and fully in command.

However, he had not become handsome and there was no reason for Brianna to experience such a shiver of awareness at his touch. And to feel so attracted by his masculine strength, to feel the desire to never leave the shelter of his arms.

While in Denver, she'd had several boyfriends, all very smart-looking and pleasant to be with. But she had not felt this powerful attraction for any one of them.

Sighing, she leaned against him, with her head on his shoulder. Nice. She was ready to explore this new feeling and to anticipate being in his arms more often. She didn't know why he was protesting, but she was sure she could convince him to explore this attraction together.

Her flowery smell was intoxicating. Virgil buried his nose in her hair and inhaled deeply. "Brianna, what are you doing? I told you before not to toy with me."

"I'm just dancing, Virgil, relax."

No, he could not relax. Nights filled with dreams of her, of holding her like that in his arms and unleashing the passion he'd held inside for so long, made him pull her closer. Just then, the song ended and Virgil decided he'd had enough dancing for one night. "We're going home," he announced, guiding her toward the exit.

It was very cold outside and surprisingly the sky was clear. A myriad of stars twinkled above the Laramie high plateau.

"Look Virgil! The sky is so beautiful. It's like it is competing with the town in decorating for Christmas with thousands of lights," Brianna said, looking up. "You

VIVIAN SINCLAIR

know, when I was a little girl I had a secret place in the barn loft where I could see far away and look at the stars at night through a little window. I bet tonight would be quite a view from there."

Virgil pulled her in his arms and kissed her with all the passion that he had worked so hard to restrain until then. Instead of pushing him away, she circled his neck with her arms and pulled closer, opening to him.

How long the kiss lasted, Virgil couldn't say, but he felt her shiver and he pulled back. "You are cold," he said when reality penetrated his foggy mind and some strident laughter from farther away broke his passionate intent. "I'm sorry. Let's get you inside my truck."

"Virgil, if you apologize one more time for kissing me, I'm going to… fire you," Brianna said, getting in the truck.

Once behind the wheel, Virgil turned to her. "As I said, you can't fire me. Only Tom can. But you'll be happy to know that I intend to go away after the New Year."

She waved her hand at him. "Nonsense. I was

146

joking. Besides I was a very active participant, so why are you apologizing?"

He started driving, inscrutable in the darkness of the cab. "Why did you come back, Brianna? I understand your life was pretty good in Denver. What made you return here?"

"My father made me believe that I can't survive outside our ranch, our family, and this community in general. I had to prove to myself that I can. And I did. I also experienced all the advantages of living in a big city. It's a wonderful world out there and I had a lot of friends. But after Thanksgiving, when the city got into the frenzy of decorating and preparing for Christmas, I realized how much I missed my family and celebrating Christmas here. I missed riding far on our lands. So I had to come back. Can you understand this, Virgil?"

"Somewhat, yes."

Brianna looked at him with curiosity. She didn't know much about him. "Don't you miss your family sometimes?"

"No," he answered flatly. "I don't have a family.

My father died when I was six and there was no one else after that. I don't remember much, except his booming laughter and that he used to lift me high up in his arms and tell me that I will grow up to be that big and tall. He loved me."

"You've been alone since you were six? What about your mother?"

"My mother remarried just six months after Dad died. Did she love me? Maybe. I don't know. She was too afraid of her husband to show it."

Brianna began to have a picture of what Virgil's childhood had been. "What about Christmas? Didn't you celebrate it like any other family?"

"No. My mother's husband considered it frivolous spending. Of course, we had light strings and decorations from the years before he came to our ranch. We were not allowed to use those either, although there was no spending involved."

"I'm sorry, Virgil. Was he a harsh father?"

"He used to beat me almost every day until I could barely move."

Brianna covered her mouth with her hand to stifle her cry of horror. "Didn't your mother call the police?"

"My mother was afraid of him. She was a weak person. Can we talk about something more cheerful? Look at these houses... how prettily they are decorated." They were passing through the outskirts of town. "These are modest homes and look what effort they made to string lights along the roof and place wreaths on the doors."

"Yes, pretty," Brianna agreed distracted. She couldn't get out of her mind the pain Virgil had been through as a child. "So you ran away from home?"

He nodded. "When I was twelve. I was big for my age, so I said I was sixteen and was hired to work in construction."

"It must have been difficult for one so young," she mused.

"Difficult? Not at all. I worked for money, not for free, and I was not beaten every day. It was much better, trust me."

"Didn't you have to go to school?"

149

"No. As far as anybody knew, I was sixteen and a drop out. I was working hard. Nobody asked questions. After a couple of years, the carpenter in the team explained that I should get tutored at the local high school to get my GED. And I did."

"How did you get to work for Parker's ranch?"

"I missed working with cattle and the open space of the range. I was in Laramie when I met Parker who told me about this mysterious place, Dargill Creek, and some spooked caves there. I am very curious and I wanted to explore that place, so I looked for work there."

"Dargill Creek is said to be cursed," Brianna said. "I remember stories, local legends about it, and about our Outlaw's Rocks and the Dead Indian's Canyon. There is a kernel of truth in the legends about these places."

"It's very interesting. Although there is nothing cursed at the cave at Dargill Creek. I've been there. It is a remote, hidden place where people running from the law used to hide. People are superstitious, that's all. I talked once to Old Man Maitland. He's writing a book about the real history and legends of Southeastern Wyoming."

Virgil parked his truck behind the barn, where he usually did. He wondered if it would be presumptuous to kiss her one more time to last him through the long hours of the night. He turned to her and took his time to touch her hair, then her face like a blind man learning the profile of the dear one. "How come you don't reject me like before?" he asked before cursing himself mentally for asking such a question.

Brianna smiled in the dark. "I changed, you changed. Time went on." And she just waited there like it was very natural for him to touch her.

It was more than Virgil could take. Throwing caution to the wind, he touched her lips with his own. The kiss ignited a wildfire in both of them. Brianna moaned and pulled him closer. After feasting on her mouth he spread butterfly kisses along her jaw and tasted the sweet, sensitive skin below her ear and down her neck.

"Virgil, come with me to the barn loft. The stars are amazing from that window."

Tempting. Oh, how tempting. But Virgil knew

that next day, they'd have to face reality and with it regret. "Not a good idea, Brie. Us alone in the loft."

"Come on. There are no lights in the bunkhouse. The others are not back yet," she argued.

Virgil didn't say that the others probably wouldn't be back until the next day. He hoped Travis had driven Maggie safely home before drowning himself in a seedy bar.

"Come," Brianna said again and got out assuming as always that she'd be followed. She walked to the barn.

What could Virgil do but go after her and up the ladder into the loft. It was not that he didn't try to make her see reason. He tried, didn't he?

The sky was indeed spectacular, seen through the little window. It was quite a sight indeed, Virgil thought. But Brianna dropped her coat on the hay and then her sweater, so Virgil got distracted. She shivered so he took her in his arms.

The moment when she saw the scars on his back was as awkward as he expected. She cried in distress and he grabbed his shirt to cover himself. Brianna stopped him and proceeded to kiss his back soothing the painful memories brought back by the long ago healed wounds.

He pulled her back to him and showed her his passion and his desire for her, everything that he was unable to say with words.

CHAPTER 15

Travis saw Virgil walking out with Brianna and thought that if the young girl was in love with him, she'd have a big heartache. Maggie was nestled in his arms with her head on his shoulder, swaying gently to the slow music. He touched gently her short hair. She was both strong and oddly vulnerable. Travis felt for her a deep affection and the desire to protect her from the disappointments unavoidable in life. Not a good idea for a man like him. A drifter, with no home of his own, had no business getting attached, not even to a dog. A delicate, young girl like Maggie was out of the question.

It was true that a man felt lonely sometimes and did foolish things in his old age. He even started to think that in fact he had a home base that he'd not visited for quite a while.

The song ended and Travis pulled Maggie to the side of the hall. The number of people had dwindled down and only a few slightly inebriated people were gyrating and clapping their hands on the dance floor. It was late and Travis had to take Maggie home.

"Oh, I had a great time," Maggie said laughing. "Did Virgil leave?" she asked looking around.

"Yes, he left a while ago," Travis answered pulling her closer to him to avoid a swaying cowboy who collapsed near them on one of the tall stools in front of the bar.

Maggie looked over her shoulder and placed her arm around Travis' waist trustingly. He felt like the Big Bad Woolf, but he was all she had at the moment.

"It's time to get you home, Maggie."

"Too bad. I had fun." She collected her coat and the lavender cap with assorted scarf and gloves. She was so cute. He bent and kissed her laughing mouth. Her lips tasted so sweet, and addictive. He almost kissed her again before he came to his senses. The huge muscular bouncer was looking at him with suspicion.

He grabbed Maggie's hand and they made their way outside. The sky was clear and Maggie continued to laugh and twirled around a lamppost. It reminded him again of how impossible his dreams were and how young and innocent she was. He was a jaded failure of a cowboy, too old and completely unsuitable to her. Better just to drive her home and leave it at that.

"Maggie, do you love Virgil?" he heard himself asking despite his resolution to steer clear of her.

She stopped twirling and the smile froze on her lips – or so it seemed to Travis. She was serious all of a sudden. "Virgil is a very special person and yes, I love him. He practically saved my life two years ago."

"I know, your brother…"

"My stepbrother was involved in a lot of illegal stuff, a bank robbery, kidnapping, running from the law. I had no idea and he never told me what he was doing at the time. He had been my legal guardian and my only living relative. He tried to drag me into his business. When he was caught, I was with him. Virgil was the only one who understood that I was innocent and he persuaded rancher Parker not to accuse me of the same crimes as my stepbrother. He showed me mercy and support. He also explained that I could take my GED and that it was up to me to make something of my life."

"You could be grateful for all this, but gratitude is not the same as love," Travis observed.

"He's the only man I trust and I know he is good and hard-working. What's there not to love?"

Her reasoning puzzled Travis. Luckily for him Maggie clarified, "I know he is in love with his Boss' sister. The entire county knows. But she went away and I thought Virgil was as lonely as I was and we could spend some time together. She came back. End of story. But we remained friends. Or so I thought." She frowned. "I don't know Brianna at all. But I wish Virgil all the happiness in the world. He deserves to be happy. And if she is what makes him happy, then I hope she'll be good to him."

Life was complicated and poor Virgil's was bound to be even more, considering Brianna's unpredictability. Not to mention the person who had attempted on his life three times now, Travis thought.

The cab of the truck finally warmed up, although Maggie didn't seem fazed by the cold despite having her legs encased in thin stockings and short boots and her skirt didn't cover her knees. Travis considered offering her the blanket he had in the back, and then thought better of it. If a woman wanted to show off her legs – and what pretty legs those were – it wouldn't do to suggest covering them.

"I love Christmastime," Maggie said, looking at all the houses festively lighted and the decorations in the windows. "Some consider it too commercial, but in the dead of winter, it makes life more cheerful and people happier, anticipating this celebration with gifts and all the trims."

"I wouldn't know. I never had a proper Christmas celebration."

"How so? Didn't your parents celebrate it?"

The truck stopped in front of the small house where Maggie rented a room. Travis considered not answering and just taking her to the door. But her gorgeous blue eyes were full of curiosity about him.

"I was an orphan, Maggie. I was left on the front steps of St. Magdalene church in Denver. The two nuns who found me wanted to baptize me Madeline until they discovered I was a boy. The nuns were upset I was not a proper Madeline. They had their heart set on this name, you see. They had an old janitor who was cleaning the place. When the janitor came in with his brooms, one of the sisters told him, 'Not now, Travis.' Then they looked at each other and Travis was my name."

Maggie was laughing and crying in the same time. She cupped his cheek. "You're a good man, Travis. Tell me more about yourself."

"My life was not exciting. I lived in a string of foster care homes, some better than others. Money was scarce. There were no Christmas celebrations, but at least there was no abuse. Sometimes we were yelled at and ordered around, but no beatings. I'm grateful for that. I was on my own at eighteen."

Still holding her hand on his cheek, Maggie looked at him. "Were you really a rodeo champion?"

"I never told you I was. I think other men talked about it. Yes, I won quite my share of competitions. I had to. I paid my college tuition with my earnings."

"I'm taking some classes at the community college too and I hope in a couple of years to get an associate degree in Veterinary Technology and be a vet assistant." Maggie nestled near him and Travis placed his arm around her shoulders. It was getting colder in the truck with the engine off. But both of them were reluctant to end their night together. "So did you finish college?" she asked.

"Yes, I did. By then I was earning much more in rodeo prizes than by working a desk job. So I said to myself, I'll do it for a few more years only, to have enough money to buy a place of my own." Travis paused surprised he'd told her that much about himself. What happened in recent times was ugly and he wanted to spare her that. But she was a curious little girl and wanted to know. He saw it in her eyes. Whatever good opinion she had of him would vanish. He hated to see her disappointed in him.

What could he do? He kissed her one more time, to satisfy his cravings of her sweet lips and discovered once was not enough. How could he make such a mess of everything? He'd had a lot of women on the rodeo circuit and their pleasant but temporary company had been enough. Why did he feel this need for this slip of a girl? Was it because he was getting older? … He was fourteen years older than her.

"Maggie, let's end the night here," he said still holding her close.

"You don't like me?" she asked hesitant.

"I just kissed you senseless and I'm about to do much more if we continue. Do I look like I don't like you?"

"But you don't want to go on another date with me," she said very perceptive.

The way she braced herself for his rejection was his undoing. It would be better if she knew the truth about him than to think she was unlovable.

"I'm not worthy of you Maggie," he started.

"Let me be the judge of this, if this is the only reason," she interrupted him.

"Listen, first, it just occurred to me now that I'm fourteen years older than you. It makes me feel like a lecherous old creep when I touch you."

"Get over it. Difference in age happen frequently

with couples. It doesn't matter. It's not a reason not to give our relationship a chance. I like you very much."

He frowned. Maybe they had a chance, because he – Lord forgive him – liked her very much too. More than that, he needed her like he hadn't needed any other woman in the past.

"Wait! There is more. I was a very ambitious man. A year ago I was competing at the Nationals in Denver."

"Wow! You were at the National Championships. I thought you just followed the rodeo competitions at the local level."

Again her undeserved admiration humbled him. He dreaded to see it change, but he had to tell her the truth. "I was a good bull rider." That was an understatement. He had been the best, until…

"So, what happened?" Maggie interrupted his musings with impatience.

"I was well positioned to win and the first rounds I was lucky to get good bulls, feisty, putting up a good fight to get a high score. Not all animals presented in rodeos are like that. Some are too mellow and they don't get the rider a good score, although this doesn't happen at the Nationals. Here, the bulls are well selected. I'm telling you all these details so you'll have a clear picture. I had a friend who competed mostly in bronc riding, but that year he tried bull riding too. He needed money and he was lucky to qualify for the Nationals. In the fifth round, however, his luck went out. The draw assigned him Voracious, an eighteen thousand pound beast that was feared by all the riders and he was famous for bucking off most cowboys brave to ride him." He covered his eyes. The memories were still painful. They would always be.

"So, what happened?" Maggie asked taking his hand away from his face and holding it into her small palms.

"The night before the round, my friend told me he had decided to quit. He was not going to ride that monster bull. I thought he had a bout of jitters before competing. We all had from time to time. It was not unusual. I didn't realize that he had an anxiety attack. In my mind, I thought, yes, he was unlucky to get Voracious and if he got bucked off before the eight seconds were over, he'd get zero points, but he had to go out there to do his best and that was all. I was pushy and I convinced him to do it, against his will."

Travis covered his face. The nightmare was going to follow.

CHAPTER 16

"Did he ride that bull?"

Travis nodded. "Yes, he did. I can see it in front of my eyes like it was yesterday. He was thrown off and the bull trampled him before the rodeo clowns succeeded to distract him away. My friend was paralyzed from the waist down for life."

"Oh, Travis." Maggie had her arms around him and pulled him to her. "I bet you blame yourself and it's not right."

"Don't you understand? He didn't want to do it and I convinced him to ride," Travis said with anguish breaking his voice.

"He was an adult man and an experienced rodeo rider. This was the path he had chosen in life, to compete in rodeos. He knew there were risks and he implicitly accepted them when he decided to follow this path. He wanted to compete in the Nationals, what rider wouldn't? That was his chance...."

"Maggie, stop. He was afraid. If you climb on a

mellow bull with fear, you are doomed, but on Voracious, it is suicide. This is what happened. It was my fault."

"You didn't force him to ride that bull. You explained that this was his opportunity to win at the Nationals. He was the only one able to estimate his chances and to know his fear. Ultimately, he decided to do it, not you. I'm not trying to minimize your friend's accident. What happened to him is very unfortunate, but it was an accident. You should both go on with your lives the best you can. Have you seen him since?"

"No, of course not. How could I? He would spit in my face. And rightly so."

Maggie shook her head. "I think you're wrong. I think he would love to see you and to know that your friendship is as strong as ever."

The first instinct was to disagree. But what if it was true? What if Johnny wanted to see him? Travis remembered that he had received a few emails from him, but he had been afraid to read them. Maybe Maggie was right and somehow seeing Johnny would be cathartic for both of them.

"What did you do after that?" Maggie asked, knowing that Travis' life had been turned upside down.

"I quit the competitions. These Nationals were supposed to be my last rodeo. I was old and with a lot of broken bones. It was time to let younger guys have their chance. I was burned out. It was a no-brainer to quit after Johnny's accident. Then I started having nightmares and a guilty conscience. I discovered that although the previous year I had bought a place for myself in Texas, I couldn't find peace there. I couldn't find peace anywhere. I couldn't compete in rodeos. I started drifting from place to place, keeping mostly to myself and working as a cowhand. A gipsy, this is what I am. Never too long in one place or people will start asking questions I am not willing to answer. Worse, I might get too friendly, like I did with Virgil."

"Virgil will never judge you. I know he thinks like I do. You have to see your friend and get over your guilt. Life is too short to be wasted by only existing instead of fully experiencing it."

"Since when did you become a philosopher, Miss Maggie," he said ruffling her hair.

"Since my mother died and my father left for parts unknown. I had to push my way through life. Now, Travis, as I said before, I like you and I'd like to date you." She scrunched up her nose. "This approach was not very successful with Virgil, but I swear if you tell me you have a secret unrequited love hidden somewhere, I'll scratch her eyes out."

He laughed. "No. No secret love, no hidden wife. I'm amazed you still want me after everything that I told you."

"We all have baggage. Nobody is perfect. I come with a stepbrother in jail and a confused time in high school when I dropped out. I also come with a GED and a good plan for the future," she added with pride. "You are a good man, Travis," she repeated.

"How can you be sure?"

"Virgil thinks so and he said you saved his life. Is it true?"

"Some people were playing with a rifle on the

range and I pushed him to the ground. Nothing spectacular." Maybe there was more to it when he found Virgil sprawled in the middle of the road with a maniac holding a shovel above his head ready to strike, but there was no sense in alarming Maggie. Travis intended to watch over Virgil carefully and in the end they had to catch the intruder.

Maggie studied him with interest. "Do you know I was attracted to you from the first time I saw you?"

His jaw dropped in surprise. "I thought you weren't. On the contrary, I thought you disliked me. You smiled at all the cowboys coming with more or less invented animal ailments and you frowned whenever you saw me. You got two little creases right here." He touched her forehead.

"That is because I thought you were conceited and lied about being a rodeo champion. Many cowboys are like that. I didn't care about the others, but I was upset about you."

"I never lied and I don't think I ever said anything to you about being a rodeo champion."

"True. Come to think of it, the others talked about your trophies. Virgil told me that they are real."

"Would you like a rodeo champion?"

"No. I would like a man who doesn't lie. Frankly I haven't met many. Only Virgil."

She was adorable, so full of righteous indignation. Travis forgot their discussion and kissed her. She leaned her head on the top of the seat and pulled him closer. The passion in their kiss could have steamed the truck's windows. He pulled back when a dog barking in the neighborhood reminded Travis of where they were.

"I'm too old to make love in the truck."

Maggie touched his face again. She was a toucher, not that he was complaining. "About that ... hmm, I have to warn you I don't have too much experience," she proclaimed, looking at him anxiously.

It took some time for Travis to understand. In the rodeo world, the women following the trail were all experienced, sometimes even more than the young guys who had just started to compete. "Are you telling me that you have never made love before?"

"Yeah. Something like that. I was planning to ask Virgil to … do it. What with him being in love with someone else, I figure he won't do it."

Travis covered her mouth with his hand. "I'll kill him if he touches you. You are mine Maggie."

"Well, okay then. Of course, I wouldn't like Virgil killed."

It was true. Sometime during this night of talking, he had decided that whatever course his life would take, Maggie was his. He needed her and he'd do whatever was necessary to keep her.

"I have to go now," Maggie said with regret. "I'll see you tomorrow."

"Tomorrow," he parroted confused.

"In church," she clarified.

"We're getting married tomorrow?" he asked, blinking owlishly. Not a bad idea. After all, he'd acted often on the spur of the moment and not all his actions had ended badly. Marrying Maggie seemed like a bright idea. In fact, the more he thought about it, the better it sounded.

She laughed like a tinker bell sound to his ears. "No, silly. Tomorrow is Sunday. We're going to church for the Sunday sermon."

He didn't mention that it had been a long time since he'd been to church. "Yes. We'll see each other in church tomorrow," he agreed eagerly. If Maggie wanted to go to church, then he'd get dressed in his Sunday best and meet her there. Maybe the sinner in him needed advice and absolution. "But when are we getting married?"

"Travis, we'll court properly, get to know each other, and then we'll talk about marriage."

If she wanted courting, then he had to do it properly. Women placed a lot of importance on courting.

"Very well. Courting it is. I hope it's not going to take too long. I'm too old to freeze my bones every night in the truck, not to mention we can't kiss properly here. A week of courting should be enough."

Still smiling, Maggie leaned into him and kissed him Good-bye and that took some more time delightfully spent.

CHAPTER 17

Virgil had a nice dream. He had Brianna in his arms. How many times had he dreamed this, only to wake up disappointed and alone in his bunk bed at the sound of Tiny Pete snoring?

He felt something sharp in his shoulder and a sweet flowery smell tickling his nostrils. Flowery? It couldn't be Travis' socks. He opened his eyes. A small lantern lighted the place and memories came flooding back. The loft in the barn. Brianna. He tightened his arms around her.

"Mmm…" She stretched like a cat. "Is it morning yet?"

"Morning? I hope not." They had to get dressed fast and go back to where they belonged. Virgil looked through the tiny window. A lot of stars. Still night then. Good. He grabbed the piece of sharp straw that was bothering his shoulder.

"Virgil, look at me," she asked.

It was true. He was afraid to see in her eyes the

disappointment that she'd spent the night with him, ugly Virgil. "Are you sorry, Brie?"

Sorry? She was not sorry. On the contrary, she felt wonderful. Who'd have believed that Virgil could be such a tender and skilled lover? "No, Virgil. How could I be sorry?" She smiled at him and he read the truth in her eyes. She had enjoyed their night together as much as he had.

"I love you, Brie," he said, offering her his heart that had belonged to her since the first moment he'd seen her. Then he got worried. Was it too early to tell her that he loved her? He was just a simple man and Brianna was now a sophisticated city-girl. Maybe it was a mistake. Tom had told him not to wear his heart on his sleeve.

"I know," she said still smiling. But she didn't return his love declaration, which made him feel uncomfortable.

Don't think about it Virgil, he told himself. She'd given herself to him. That had to count for something. That was a definite progress from the time when she rebuffed him.

"Virgil, we need to talk," Brianna said when she was dressed and ready to go. "Please, stay here with me a few minutes. There is at least another two hours before dawn."

"Yes, of course. You know I always wanted to marry you. Before, I couldn't afford it. Now that Tom named me foreman, it is possible. And I have some money set aside from the time when I worked in construction."

"Virgil, I'm not talking about marriage. I have some plans and I want to talk to you about them. I talked to Tom and I intend to buy a small ranch of my own and raise goats."

"Goats?" Virgil asked shocked. "But we are cattlemen."

"It's a prejudice. I would need more land for cattle and I can't afford it. I'm going to raise goats to make cheese. Goat cheese is in high demand in the restaurant industry."

"But you don't know anything about raising goats," Virgil pointed out.

"We'll learn; you and I together. I want you to come with me and be my partner. I need a hard-working man I can trust. You'll see it can work and we'll make this a success."

Virgil shook his head. This was not what he thought the morning after their night of love would be. He knew she didn't love him and thought that perhaps in time she might come to care for him. But this … proposition showed that she didn't care for him at all and never would. That for her he was only – as she'd said – a hard-working man. Oh how disappointing! He was a fool to imagine that he'd changed into a good-looking man and that any woman would look at him other than with the purpose of using him for hard work.

He was sure she'd enjoyed their love making. It had not been all pretend on her part. But she would never see him as a man to love, worthy of her heart.

He thought that if she accepted him, his love for her would be enough to make their marriage work. It showed how naïve he'd been to think she meant to marry him just because they'd made love.

Perhaps later he might accept such a partnership, but now he was too hurt. And he also realized that after a lifetime of loneliness, he needed someone in his life to love him, just one person in the world for whom he would matter, one person to return his love and devotion.

Now he understood that Brianna was not that person. He felt that his heart would break. It was much worse than last year when she'd run away with that no-good cowboy. Then, he still had hoped that she'd come back and see the truth. There was no hope now. He'd lost his dream.

Virgil closed his eyes, wishing he could make his tears disappear.

Finally he turned to her. "I'm sorry Brianna, but if I have to choose a job, for the moment I'll stay with Tom as I promised him. After the New Year, I'll search for something else. Maybe I'll go back to work in construction for a while. Money is good there."

Now it was her turn to be stunned. "Are you turning me down? You don't understand. I'm offering you a partnership, not just to be foreman. Of course, in the beginning, there will not be much money. But I know a lot of people in the restaurant industry and I'm fairly sure I can sell the cheese fast."

"I understand. It's not about the money." Truth was that if she loved him he could go through any hardship life would place in front of them, he could live dirt poor.

"But why? You don't believe I can succeed?"

He looked at her with sadness. "I believe you can succeed if you want to. It is going to be difficult, but you have what it takes to succeed."

She beamed at his praise. "Then you should agree to become my partner."

"No, Brie, I can't."

"Look, we are both reasonable people. I am ready to accept your decision if you help me understand it."

"We want different things in life."

"How so? I'm sure we both want a successful business. Where is the difference?"

Virgil looked at the starry night. It was becoming less dark now. Soon the sky would turn red in the east with the rising sun. He felt drained and empty. How could he explain to her what was important to him in life? Would she understand? "Brie, if I'd wanted money, I'd have stayed in construction. I chose to be a cowboy because I was born on a ranch and the wide open spaces called me back, just like they called you back when you were in Denver. It's hard work, but it gives me a feeling of freedom that doesn't exist anywhere else."

"That is exactly what I'm offering you. Not only the freedom of a ranch, but also to build a business of our own. Don't you see? We have the same goals," she interrupted him impatiently.

She was so beautiful, eyes flashing, determined to convince him and get her way. For a second, Virgil was tempted to bend to her wishes. So what if she didn't love him, they'd be partners. A feeling of sadness and loss enveloped him. No, it would destroy him little by little to see her smiling at other men and in the end choosing a good-looking guy and leaving him without a second thought, as she did before. He shook his head.

"Why are you so adamant? You said you loved

me, you said…" Hmm, what else did he say? Something about… oh, yes, marriage…, Brianna remembered. Quite a step to take in life. Marriage was forever, a serious commitment. Was she ready for it? Virgil was not bad as husband material, serious, loyal, reliable. And she was thirty already. Marriage was not on her mind now, but how long was she going to wait? And wait for what? She knew Prince Charming didn't exist. The pretty ones were conceited and false. And in general every person had his own agenda.

"Very well, Virgil. I accept your marriage proposal. You see I'm totally committed to our partnership in business and in life," she said, without hesitation. That was Brianna. Once she made up her mind, she pursued her objective with tenacity. Unfortunately in this case, her words did not have the desired effect. Instead of jumping up with joy and taking her in his arms to kiss her, he shook his head again and looked at her with sorrow.

"Brie, I love you. I've always loved you, even when you rejected me. I had hopes. But you can't say the same, and you shouldn't say it because it would not be true. You are too honest to pretend affection when there is none."

"Not true. I feel a lot of affection for you. I don't know if it's love. There were so many changes in my life recently, new decisions, discovering how much I like to dance with you, and then… this night together. All these are a bit much for me." Brianna paused and took a deep breath. "I'm not confused, but I am a bit dizzy. I am plowing my way into a new reality…"

"What new reality, Brie? You've always known I love you."

"Yes, I knew, but I also found a stranger determined to push me away at all cost. And I was talking about my feelings. The fact that we have so much chemistry that we could ignite the barn. Do I love you? I don't know. The feeling is too new for me."

"Sexual attraction is natural between two adults, but it is not love." Yep, Virgil thought. It was all or nothing. "It's daylight. We have to go. The others will be here soon."

Brianna stomped her foot in frustration. They needed to talk, but not now. They'd have no privacy after the others came. Virgil led her outside and to the ranch house. No more words were spoken. But at the door, Brianna grabbed Virgil by the collar of his jacket and gave him a last kiss to remember her. It was a promise that she'd not given up. Then she entered the house closing the door and leaving Virgil baffled. He thought she understood that without love there would be nothing between them. Stubborn woman.

At the bunkhouse, he came face to face with Tiny Pete who was trying to take off his boots before entering so as not to make noise. He slipped on a patch of icy snow and fell.

"You old fool, why are you taking off your boots here?" Virgil asked, giving him a hand to help him get up.

"I thought you guys were sleeping and I didn't want to disturb you. My consideration was for nothing," Tiny Pete replied.

"Why? Do you think you're the only Romeo

tiptoeing back here at the crack of dawn?"

"Who are the others?" Tiny Pete asked with interest, twirling his moustache. "By the way, Cory left with two rodeo cowboys. They were telling him all sorts of inflated stories about the glorious days in rodeo and he was gobbling it all up. The boy is chomping at the bit to break his bones in rodeo."

Virgil stopped with his hand on the door. "I thought Travis disabused him of how wonderful it is to compete in rodeo."

"Yeah, but he's young and full of energy. I bet one of these days he'll say Good-bye and leave to try his luck."

Tiny Pete opened the door and motioned for Virgil to enter the bunkhouse.

CHAPTER 18

Angel was not in the bunkhouse and Virgil was afraid that, as it was his habit, the mountain man had spent the night in the barn with the animals. Nothing wrong with that. If he'd seen them in the loft, or if he'd heard them, Virgil was sure that Angel was the person least inclined to gossip. However, it was a little unnerving that there had been a person in the barn.

Cory had probably come in late and was still snoring away the sleep of the innocents, oblivious to the noise around him.

Travis, an early riser from his rodeo days, was trying on a slightly wrinkled dark suit and frowning mightily.

"Well, look here, somebody died and we didn't know it," Tiny Pete chuckled in complete disregard to the observation he'd made. In the close confines of the bunkhouse, he was emanating a strong mixture of cologne and alcohol. Sitting on his bed, he was attempting to take off his boots.

Travis turned and very seriously said, "Nobody died. Today is Sunday and I'm going to church. This is my Sunday best."

Tiny Pete could not have been more amazed if he'd announced he was going to the moon. "What brought this on? I'm not saying your black soul doesn't need some cleaning and repentance, but I don't think this ever bothered you before."

"Repentance?" Before Travis could answer, Virgil caught him by the lapels of his suit, wrinkling it even more. "What did you do to Maggie?"

"Hey! Calm down. The question is 'what did she do to me?'. I tell you, Maggie is one determined lady."

"Aren't they all?" Tiny Pete interfered.

Travis pushed Virgil's hands away and tried ineffectively to smooth the newly acquired wrinkles in his suit. "She made me see that I have some adjustments to do if I want to live a normal life."

"Normal by whose standards?" Tiny Pete asked.

Travis ignored him. "It was all very innocent, and I slept here during the night, which is more than you can say, Mr. Holier-than-thou. Where were you last night, if I may ask?"

"You may not," Virgil answered curtly dropping on his bed.

"Heh heh, heh - he doesn't have much to say, judging by his bad mood. As for me, I had a grand night with Widow Krammer." Tiny Pete boasted very pleased with himself.

"You'd better watch out. Widow Krammer is notorious for trying to lasso any cowboy that comes her way," Travis observed. "In no time at all, you'll find yourself dressed in a dark suit in church and for grander purposes than attending Sunday service."

Virgil was usually amused by the good-natured bickering in the bunkhouse, but today he felt unsettled. "Where is Angel?" he asked.

"How should I know? Probably in the barn. Where else?"

"I thought so," Virgil muttered and went out to the barn. The mountain man often had deep insight and good advice.

A VISITOR FOR CHRISTMAS

"Virgil!" shouted two little boys climbing all over him. Wyatt Jr. and Billy were eight and six years of age respectively. They were as rambunctious as the day Virgil had met them.

"How are you two scamps doing?" he asked lifting them high up, first one, then the other, and making them laugh.

"Virgil, we have to tell you something," Wyatt said.

"It's a secret," shouted the other as loud as he could.

A secret. That sounded ominous indeed.

"What have you two done?" Virgil asked this time seriously.

"We were playing near the creek yesterday," Wyatt said.

"I thought your Dad said not to go by yourselves that far from the house," Virgil interrupted him.

Billy raised his finger. "He said 'not farther than the creek'." Of the two, he was the one who liked precise details. Lord help Tom when these two will grow up to be teenagers.

Wyatt waved his hand. "We were there because we wanted to build a fort in the snow and the snow is more abundant there. So while we were there, this man came out of nowhere. He had no horse or truck, and he wanted to talk about you."

"He was not nice. His smile was like this," Billy said and demonstrated, showing all his teeth in a large grimace, a good imitation of a Dracula Halloween mask.

"He was old. Maybe even older than you," Wyatt concluded assessing Virgil for comparison.

"He wanted to know all sorts of things about you, but don't worry, we didn't tell him the truth."

"We told him that you are married, live in town with a woman, have ten children, and that you come here only from time to time."

Virgil laughed shaking his head. The boys had imagination. But it was also scary that the man who wanted to harm him had come so close to the house and to Tom's family.

A VISITOR FOR CHRISTMAS

"He said that you have something he wants and that it was his by right and he has something of yours. And that you will trade. He's coming for you," Wyatt said carefully scrunching up his face in concentration to remember exactly.

Virgil wanted to press them for more details when a dusty truck with Texas license plates stopped in front of the house.

"Grandpa!" the boys shouted and ran toward the older man who got down from the truck. Sam Donovan claimed he was a man of the earth and didn't like flying, so he preferred to drive across half the country instead of getting into an airplane.

He opened his arms wide and bent down to hug his two precious grandsons. For a long time, he'd thought that he'd lost them. It was a miracle that his daughter-in-law and her new husband were such nice people and not only allowed the boys to come to Texas in the summers, but also included him in the warm circle of their family.

"Grandpa, did Santa come to you?"

"Did he give you gifts for us?"

They peppered him with questions.

"Have you two been good this year?" he asked. They nodded solemnly. "Did you listen to your mother and obey her?"

"Yes, we sure did. We knew you were going to ask this before giving us the gifts." They looked at him full of innocence. Billy had his son's eyes. It reminded him of his late son so much it always brought tears to his eyes.

"Well, then you can have them on Christmas morning."

"Can we place them under the tree?"

Virgil looked at the trailer hooked to the truck and knew by the sounds inside that the colt would be not only difficult to place under the tree, but also difficult to keep in the barn until Christmas without the boys noticing.

He laughed at the older rancher. "Hi Mr. Donovan. Good to see you again. The boys could hardly wait for you to arrive."

The Texan extended his hand to shake his.

A VISITOR FOR CHRISTMAS

"Virgil, I heard you were promoted to foreman. It was about time, considering all the good work you've done here."

"Thank you, sir."

"Call me Sam. I keep reminding you. We don't stand on formalities. How could we? You're the man who brought down my son's killer. I'm not about to forget it. I'm grateful to you. If for whatever reason you have a hankering to move away from here, don't forget you'll always be welcome in Texas. You'll always have a place at my ranch. Think about it. Texas is beautiful and not as cold as Wyoming."

Laughter sounded in the doorway and Tom Gorman came out to welcome his sons' grandfather. "You're just saying this because you want to steal my foreman. Welcome to Diamond G, Sam."

"Ah, we have a visitor for Christmas," Lottie said coming out too, wiping her hands on her apron.

"What visitor, Lottie? This old coot is part of the family. Come in. And Virgil, you may come too. I think we are too late for church anyway. Let's have brunch.

It's Sunday, after all."

Virgil was thinking of an excuse when Lottie pulled him inside. What could he do? He joined the family at the table. Brianna was seated at the other side of the long farm table, near her brother Chris, who was looking amused at Virgil, and winked at him. Did anybody here know his business? He was a private man, not that he'd had many secrets to hide until now.

The table was covered with food, all sorts of fancy dips and veggies that women preferred, but also slices of roast beef and ham cut thin, freshly baked bread, and a platter with cheese taquitos. Lottie was overfeeding them as usual. But nobody objected. It was Christmastime after all. The music of the season could be heard throughout the house.

At some point, Lottie placed in front of him a plate of muffins. Ah, almond and poppyseed, his favorite. They looked a bit lopsided, but Lottie was cooking a lot these days and not everything could be perfect. Although, it usually was and everything tasted delicious. He was sure his favorite muffins were great.

A VISITOR FOR CHRISTMAS

He bit into one of the muffins, anticipating the familiar bitter-sweetness of the almonds and the crunchiness of the poppyseeds. He stopped chewing. The taste was different. The almond essence was a bit overpowering and there were very few poppyseeds. The texture was not so fluffy. He chewed some more. Overall, the taste was not bad. A bit more robust. Hmm, good.

He looked to the other end of the table and swallowed. Brianna was watching him with anxiety. It dawned on him right then that she had baked the muffins. Lottie, bless her, must have told Brianna that these were his favorite and advised her to bake them for him. It was a surprise that Brianna agreed to bake them, that she took the time to learn to do it right, and that they were edible. That was a surprise.

He was impressed. Brianna had done this for him. She had cared enough about him not to let them burn as it was her habit when she was in the kitchen. Darn, just when he thought he'd pegged her right and decided they had no chance at happiness, she changed his mind.

He smiled his endearing lopsided smile and

nodded at her in acknowledgement. "Good," he mouthed at her.

CHAPTER 19

Virgil followed Brianna to her room. He wrapped his large hands around her waist and twirled her around.

"You baked the muffins for me. I can't believe it. Only Lottie ever baked or knitted especially for me, but she does that for all of us. She makes sure that we have our favorite foods and that we are bundled up when we go outside. Tom is a lucky man. I'm impressed, Brie, that you took the time to learn what I like and to bake the muffins. Did you learn to cook in Denver?"

She laughed. "No, there was no time. I only ate take out food there."

"Then, I'm surprised the muffins were so good." Virgil pulled her closer and kissed her forehead, then her eyelids, and trailed down to her lips.

"Were they?" she asked breathless.

After the first kiss, Virgil was distracted, and he didn't remember what they were talking about. Ah, right, the muffins. "Yes, they were good. In a different way than Lottie's; they had more texture, but they were delicious. Thank you."

"You're most welcome," Brianna answered, her hands busy unbuttoning his shirt.

Regretfully, Virgil covered her hand with his own to stop her. "I have to talk to Tom. He's waiting for me. It's important. But I'll be back." He stole another kiss and left the room before he could get distracted again.

He smiled hearing peals of childish laughter from the family room. Sam was telling the two boys a story from his youth in Texas, making them laugh. Most of it was probably fabricated. But who cared? They were having a grand time together. The boys loved their grandfather.

Virgil knocked briefly and entered Tom's office. Tom was looking at the computer screen. There was a plate filled with colorful cupcakes and two mugs with steaming coffee in front of him on the desk. He inclined his head and motioned for Virgil to help himself.

Virgil didn't share his boss' fondness for cupcakes, but he cheered up seeing the coffee. A good, hot coffee was always welcome on cold winter days.

A VISITOR FOR CHRISTMAS

He took a seat in front of the desk with the mug cradled in his hands. "Well Boss, we have a problem and I'm afraid it's all my fault."

Tom raised his eyes from the screen and looked at Virgil. "What problem? I mean we always have a heap of them, but to which problem are you referring?"

"The boys, Wyatt and Billy, told me that they were playing in the snow near the creek…"

"What? They are not allowed to go near the creek. I told them specifically."

"Billy mentioned that you said not to go beyond the creek. Besides, when you were their age, how many times wasn't the temptation to explore stronger than your father's good advice? Anyhow, they were building a fort and they assured me that the snow down near the creek was better for this purpose."

"A fort? What happened to the good, old snowman?"

Virgil shrugged. "Not interesting enough. So, while they were there, a stranger came to them and asked them a lot of questions about me. He was old, probably even older than me - they informed me. This man gave them a message for me. That I have something that belongs to him and that he has something I want and that he'll come for me."

"It sounds ominous. Do you think it's the same person who shot at you and who attempted to harm you?"

"Yes, it must be, unless I acquired an army of enemies overnight. It makes me shiver to think that the boys were in danger. That crazy man is after me for some reason that escapes me. He could have harmed them or kidnapped them. I would never forgive myself if something happened to them because of me. Perhaps I should go away and let him confront me elsewhere."

"No," Tom was adamant. "I think we have to let the others know that we have an intruder and to watch out, to be vigilant and aware of danger. But it is Christmas and I refuse to let this spoil our enjoyment of the celebration. As for the boys, they'll be with Sam. The Texan is a force to reckon with and a fierce fighter. I remember him from last year. He'll protect the kids."

A VISITOR FOR CHRISTMAS

"I swear to you, Tom, I have no idea who this man is and why he's after me. I don't fight in bars. I'm not a hothead, not easy to rile or quick to exchange words or fists. I own nothing of value and I don't have anything that belongs to someone else."

"I believe you and I know it's true. But ..."

The door opened and Lottie came in smiling. "Hey guys, we have a visitor for Christmas."

Tom looked at his wife with amusement. "Who is it this time, Lottie? I know you're happy to have people around you for Christmas."

A tall man entered after her. He was in his sixties, but still strong and well built. He looked from Tom to Virgil, and then reaching a conclusion, he nodded satisfied. "I'm Virgil Townsend and I'm a lawyer from Missoula, Montana."

Virgil jumped from his chair. "What? You can't be. My name is Virgil Townsend."

"In that case, I am your uncle Gil from Missoula. I don't think you remember me, but you were named after me."

"After my father passed away, my mother told me we had no other family," Virgil said confused.

"When my brother died so suddenly, we were all grieving. By the time I thought to offer help to your mother with the ranch, she was already remarried. I talked to your stepfather a year later and he let me know in no uncertain terms that he is in charge and that his family wanted nothing to do with me. I called a few years later to ask about you and I talked to your mother who said that you were gone. She started crying and hung up. I thought you had passed away. I mourned your loss, even though it had been years since I'd seen you."

Tom, who had been silent until now, invited the newcomer to take a seat and offered him his precious cupcakes. "It's very unfortunate when family members become estranged due to various circumstances. Please, help yourself. My wife loves to cook and to see people enjoy her food. Virgil is my foreman, but we consider him part of our family. Tell me what prompted you to come to look for him now, after all these years?"

The lawyer bit into one of the chocolate cupcakes

and rolled his eyes with pleasure. "Oh man! This is good!" He swallowed, and then continued his story. "Your mother contacted me last year. She was very sick and knew she was dying. The disease was incurable and it was very advanced. I'm sorry."

Virgil thought of the small bundle left near the barn door many years ago. She had been a weak woman, and he was not sure if she'd ever loved him like his father had. But she did the best she could to let him run away and help with the very little that she had. That had saved his life.

The lawyer - Virgil had a hard time calling him uncle – started to talk again. "I have to explain that your father had no will when he died. He was a young man and he never expected to die so young. According to the law in Montana, the surviving spouse received all his property. Your mother became the sole owner of the ranch. Her new husband tried to force her to transfer the property to him, but she resisted. However, he made her write a will with him as the sole beneficiary in case of her death."

"Oh, Lord." Virgil wiped his brow. The emotion was choking him.

"As I said, she came to me a year ago and told me everything. How she lived in fear all these years, how helpless she felt when her new husband was beating you for at every real or imagined mistake you made. And finally, how she knew you were big and strong enough to run away and accepted this because she saw no other way to save you."

"I was twelve," Virgil scoffed, remembering that the fear that his stepfather would come after him had been greater than the fear of going into the unknown at such a young age. Nightmares had plagued him every night for years.

"I'm sorry, son. Perhaps I should have taken a more forceful approach and come to see what was going on, to insist to see you. I was young and I had some personal difficulties at the time and I felt overwhelmed when my brother died so unexpectedly."

"What happened to Virgil's mother?" Tom asked.

"Last year, she came to see me and made a last

will in which she left all her property to Virgil, including the ranch and the house. She had a medical certification that she was sane and not coerced in this. She added specifically that her previous will was null and void and that the ranch had belonged to her first husband's family for fifty years. It was right to go to you and her second husband had no right to it."

"Oh!" Virgil swallowed hard and tried to control his emotion.

"Wait," Tom addressed to the lawyer. "What happens if Virgil were not alive?"

"But he is..." the lawyer objected, confused.

"Please humor me."

"Well, I guess, in that case his mother's property will go automatically to the only surviving relative of hers, her second husband."

"Aha," Tom exclaimed with satisfaction. "Virgil, here you have a valuable property and that man thinks it's his by right."

"You don't think he came after me?" Virgil was horrified by this possibility.

However, Tom relished this idea. "Come on, you're not a frightened twelve year old boy. I hope he is the one. You deserve a confrontation and closure." He patted Virgil on the back.

Virgil did not look forward to seeing his stepfather again. Unfortunately, the more he thought about it, the more it looked like Tom was right. He turned toward his newly acquired uncle. "What happened to Ma?"

"She died just a month after she saw me. I was very careful to record properly all the papers and when your stepfather wanted to take possession of the ranch legally, he realized he could not. He appealed, but the law is very clear and the will was iron-clad. I hired a private investigator to look for you. And here I am. Twenty years too late, I hope you'll forgive me for this, but at least now I did my legal best to right a wrong. You are the sole owner of our family ranch."

"Wow, Virgil, you are a man of property now," Tom joked. "That young filly in Laramie will be ecstatic that her boyfriend is a rancher."

A VISITOR FOR CHRISTMAS

"What filly?" the uncle asked interested.

"His girlfriend in town," Tom replied.

CHAPTER 2O

Meanwhile, the so-called girlfriend was freezing her feet in the street and cooling her temper. Maggie was waiting for Travis in front of her house. The old lady, from whom she was renting the room, had tried to persuade her that rodeo cowboys were not serious and that she was naïve to think he didn't have a girlfriend in every town. Especially an avowed drifter like Travis.

Maggie was so mad that she decided to wait for him outside. Travis was not like that. She just knew it. He was a lonely man in desperate need of true love and affection. He was so much like her. She could trust him.

Five minutes later, Travis' truck stopped at the curb. Maggie ran into his arms. "You came, you came," she repeated, jumping up and down glad to see him and perhaps to make the blood flow faster in her frozen feet.

Travis frowned. "I said I'd come, didn't I?" But he caught her in his arms and gave her a sound kiss. Her lips were cold as was the rest of her and she was shivering in her pretty, but thin jacket and with a skirt that barely covered her knees. "Get in. You're frozen."

Once inside the truck, Travis didn't start the engine. "I am not late, am I?" In fact, he thought that he'd be ridiculous showing up earlier. He was a bit rusty at this dating thing, not to mention at going to church.

"No, of course not. I waited outside and it was chillier than I thought." She looked at him. His suit had seen better days and it was wrinkled, in desperate need of ironing. But he'd come and made an effort to look presentable. This was ranching country. There were many men who came to church wearing jeans, their best and cleanest, but still jeans, not a suit. She doubted they even had one.

"Do you approve? It's all I had on such a short notice."

Maggie's blue eyes were shining like stars. "Travis, you dressed like this for me. Not only do I approve, but it warms my heart."

"Are you sure you wouldn't prefer Virgil?" His doubts were still bothering him.

"I repeat what I told you before. Virgil was the

only man I trusted and who didn't let me down. Given a chance, it's possible our friendship might have developed into something more meaningful and profound like love. But Virgil's heart is already given as he explained to me very patiently. End of story. I'm not pining for him. And I like you very much. I liked you ever since I first met you, almost a year ago, but I didn't trust you then." Maggie paused to think. She was honest and just realized that she had stereotyped Travis in the same way her landlady did. A flighty, conceited rodeo cowboy. And he was such a good-hearted man.

"All right then, I'm not going to ask again, I promise."

His dark hair was wavy and thick and she pulled his head down to her for a kiss. Later, with her head on his shoulder Maggie asked, "Travis, did you mean it when you said you want to marry me?"

He raised his head to look into her eyes. "Of course I meant it. I think I did from the first day I entered the veterinary clinic with that ornery horse that needed his leg doctored by a vet and he was showing his bad temper by trying to kick me. I was mad too, until I saw a pair of blue eyes laughing at me. A slip of a girl, with short hair and sweet voice made the horse follow her inside meek as a lamb."

"Oh, Travis. Really?"

"Really. But you see I'm much older than you. I've seen life and experienced a lot. You are young. Perhaps you need to meet other people…" He stopped.

"Would you like me to meet other men?"

When put this way, it was the most idiotic thing he could suggest. "No. I'll kill them all if they so much as touch your hand. I'll have to marry you soon."

"I'm glad you want to. Of course, it's not going to be possible," she said with regret in her voice. "Not anytime soon."

"What do you mean? You changed your mind?"

"No, I didn't. But it will take me at least two more years to get my associate degree, so I can get a better paid job. Right now, all we can have is a rented room somewhere."

That left Travis totally flabbergasted. "Maggie,

did you think I asked you to marry me without a penny in my pocket to support you?"

She smiled at him. Men's ego was indeed fragile. A girl needed to be careful not to trample it. "Look, you live in a bunkhouse with other cowboys and I rent a small room from this old lady. I don't need much and I don't fear poverty, but be reasonable and give me a little time to finish college. I'll work hard I promise."

He shook his head in wonder. "You're not listening to me. I told you that all my life I wanted a place of my own and I saved my rodeo earnings for that. I have a ranch in Texas. It's the most beautiful place on earth you've ever seen. The fact that I don't live there is because, as I've explained to you, I couldn't find peace there after my friend's accident. But you're right. It was what it was, and it's time to visit him and no matter what the outcome of this visit, it's time to make peace with myself, to forgive myself and start a new life. With you, if you'll have me."

"Yes, I'll go with you to Texas. Too bad for my degree, though," she said regretfully. Then she brightened. "Do you think I could finish my degree there? There must be some community college nearby...."

He sighed. "You can have anything you want, even a veterinary doctor's degree."

"That takes longer and costs a lot of money."

"You can have it, Maggie. Anything you want. I'll support you. Don't worry about money. I have money. Have you heard of T.A. Tremaine?"

"Sure. He was a champion bull rider, famous at the Nationals. They say there was no bull that could buck him off. Why? Do you know him?" she asked with curiosity. T.A. Tremaine was a legend. Even people not very interested in rodeos had heard of him.

"Yeah, you could say that. I'm T.A. Tremaine. I won The National Championship All Around Title five times. That ill-fated one would have been my sixth. After that, I'd planned to retire at my ranch in Texas."

"You're T.A. Tremaine?" Maggie looked at him dazed, like in a dream.

"Yep. So you see, there is no reason to worry

about money. I have plenty for a decent life on our ranch."

"Why didn't you say anything? Not to your co-workers, not to me…"

"Because I was not proud of myself. I felt guilty. And I didn't want a circus around me."

"That's why you worked like a simple ranch hand. Like some sort of penance."

Travis bent his head. "Probably, although I didn't think about it that way. I was desperate and I couldn't find peace on my own ranch. So I drifted from one place to another, working to do odd jobs or as a ranch hand. Then moving on again. Living a simple life and trying to achieve inner balance through this basic life style. Just surviving. And when people started asking more questions that I was comfortable answering, I moved on."

"Until you came here…." Maggie filled in, nestling closer in his arms.

"Until I met Virgil who decided that I was a hero for saving his life. Then he forced me to come to the dancing hall to dance with you. When you came into my life, Maggie, my melancholy had no chance."

"Oh, Travis, I can't believe you're T A Tremaine." She frowned and turned to him. "What does A stand for?"

"Nothing."

"Come on, you can tell me. I can't marry a man without knowing his middle name. How bad can it be? Archibald?" she guessed joking.

"You'll be disappointed. It's nothing. I don't have a middle name. Like a foundling, the good sisters who found me decided Tremaine rimed well with Travis and that was the extent of their imagination."

"Then where did the A came from?"

"At my first rodeo competition, the person who was writing down the names of the entries, asked for my middle initial. He had to write one or the entry was incorrect and I would not be accepted. I was a cocky young man, annoyed by the formalities, so I said 'write whatever you want, the first letter in the alphabet is A'. And that's what he wrote."

"And so a legend was born. T.A. Tremaine. You now, I like the name."

"Is it good enough to change your own to it?" he asked.

"Yes, Travis, it is."

He checked his wrist watch. "I think we are late for church."

"No, we're not. I planned to be there early, so you could meet some of the nice people in our congregation. Now we are just in time. Drive on."

They were just in time. Travis couldn't make much sense of what the pastor was saying because he was distracted by his earlier conversation with Maggie. Sitting in the pew next to her and holding her hand, gave him a feeling of peace and well-being like never before.

CHAPTER 21

The door to Tom's office suddenly opened, hitting the wall.

"What girlfriend?" Brianna asked from the doorway.

"Ah, come in, Brie. We have a surprise visitor for Christmas." Tom came from behind his desk to stand near his sister. "Come meet Mr. Virgil Townsend, a lawyer from Missoula, Montana. This is my sister, Brianna."

"Is this a joke?" she asked examining the stranger in her brother's office.

"No joke, my dear. This is Virgil's Uncle Gil," Tom explained.

"I thought Virgil had no family at all."

"He does now."

She looked at Virgil, but there was no hope there to clarify the identity of the man. Virgil himself seemed amazed to see this new visitor. She narrowed her eyes. "With all due respect, sir, you remembered after all these years that you have a nephew?"

"It's a long story," the lawyer said thinking that this was a termagant of a girl and that whoever would be the guy to win her heart, she'd lead him on a merry chase. He wondered if his newly rediscovered nephew had what it took to catch her. Rancher Gorman talked about a girlfriend in town, but Townsend, as a lawyer had to be astute and observant of details, and it was clear to him that Virgil looked at this girl like she was the greatest thing since sliced bread.

While Tom told Brianna their visitor's story, Townsend scrutinized Virgil. He was tall and well-built like his father, but he had none of the Townsends' charm. His face was plain like his mother's. Considering that the girl was a pretty brunette and the sister of a wealthy rancher, he wondered what Virgil's chances of winning her heart were. Yes, his father's ranch was large, but as they say, 'land rich, money poor'. He still had to relay to Virgil the true condition of his inheritance.

"I see," Brianna finally said when Tom finished the whole story. She looked at Virgil who was watching her. "Where is this ranch and how big is it?" she asked.

"Brie, these are details that Mr. Townsend will tell Virgil," Tom admonished her.

The lawyer chuckled. He really liked this girl and maybe with her strong personality, she was what his nephew needed. Nothing like the mealy-mouthed woman Virgil's mother had been. He still had to take Virgil's measure because he had only listened and hadn't said much.

Her brother's words didn't stop Brianna, and she opened her mouth to ask more questions. Virgil touched her hand and she looked at him and stepped back near him. All right, maybe his nephew had some personal way of communicating with her. There might be hope for him yet.

"Please tell us the details. I have no secrets from my friends here," Virgil said with a calm that he didn't feel.

The lawyer sighed. "The ranch is extensive. It was quite profitable at one time, when my parents lived, and after them, when my brother was the owner," he said answering Brianna's question. "Virgil, I wish I could give you better news, but now the ranch is only a ghost of what it once was. All that remains is the land and the old house. Everything is in ruin and the livestock was sold a long time ago. That scoundrel married to your mother sold everything he could, except the land. It will take a lot of capital to make it prosperous again. It can be done, but it will be a lot of hard work. About the money, I'll do my best to help you, but you'll need to take a loan."

Again, Virgil looked at Brianna wanting to see her reaction and she nodded in a muted agreement. For the first time, she smiled and Townsend saw how beautiful she was. The smile was directed at his nephew. "Perfect," she said clapping her hands.

"What's perfect?" her brother asked bewildered. "Of course we will help Virgil, but the situation is far from perfect."

It seemed that her brother was not aware of the vibes in the room. Would he oppose a marriage between the sister he loved – that much was obvious – and the man who was his foreman and worked for him?

"I have a perfect solution, but Virgil and I need to talk about the details,"

"Brianna," Tom cautioned her. He was aware of her impulsive decisions.

The lawyer thought a diverting intervention was necessary. "Virgil, why don't you tell me more about this girlfriend of yours?"

Maybe that was too much kindling on the fire. Virgil reddened and looked down. Brianna frowned at him. Tom was the only one unaware of the storm.

"Maggie is a wonderful girl," Tom said. "She works in a veterinarian clinic and takes classes at the community college."

"Maggie is my friend, not my girlfriend," Virgil hastened to explain. "I've known her for a long time and yes, she is a wonderful girl."

"But, Lottie said…," Tom objected.

Brianna stepped forward. "I'm his girlfriend," she said raising her chin, daring anybody to contradict her.

"Now, see here, Brie. You just returned from

Denver with lots of new ideas. Don't twist Virgil again. He has his own problems to deal with."

"Do you object to your sister being my nephew's girlfriend?" the lawyer asked curious to see what the rancher's position was.

"No, not at all. But what you don't know is that your nephew fancied himself in love with her for a long time and she would hear nothing of it. My point is - my sister is very temperamental and impulsive, acting on the spur of the moment. She's a great girl, but I'm afraid Virgil will be hurt again and nothing will come of it."

The lawyer turned to Brianna. "Well, young lady, you heard what your brother said. Are you serious about my nephew?"

"I might be impulsive, but I always finish what I start. In this case, what's between Virgil and me is our business," and saying this Brianna turned on her heel and left the room.

"That's my sister, what can I say?" Tom looked askance after her.

But Virgil smiled unfazed and Townsend

believed that perhaps there was more to his nephew than a plain face and a bland character. Any man who could handle this fiery girl must be a force to be reckoned with.

The door opened and Lottie entered. "I hope everything was explained, because we should join the others in the family room. Come to meet them."

While the others followed Lottie, Virgil went to Brianna's room. He found her there in the small window seat, absently watching the snowflakes floating down from the grey sky.

She looked up at him. "You know what I'm thinking and it is perfect."

"You want my land for the goats." He was both amused and a little sad if such a thing were possible.

She raised her chin in a gesture so like Brianna, and Virgil heart melted. "Yes, and you heard the lawyer, there is plenty of land. The ranch is large. My goats need a smaller place. We can raise cattle too. We need money to start the business and I have it. I'm impulsive and I make decisions fast, but I'm not irresponsible. I'm careful with finances. We'll start on a smaller scale and increase both operations in time, see what works and what doesn't, adjust. We can make it work." He was looking outside without answering. "What?" she asked impatiently.

He shrugged. "I don't know. Everything is weird. My uncle coming here. News that I inherited the ranch after all. It seems unreal. Then, your plans… are so business like, calculated." He turned to her. "Do you love me, Brie?"

She opened her mouth to answer, then snapped it shut. She looked at him, his craggy features so familiar. She touched his face in wonder. How could she ever have called him ugly? Perhaps he was not good-looking, but he was so dear to her. She leaned into him. She loved his strong body and his clean, masculine smell was so attractive. He was her Virgil and she knew without doubt that if he were hurt, she'd feel the pain too. She couldn't imagine life without his constant presence in it.

If this was love, then this was what she felt.

Misinterpreting her silence, he turned away from her. "Forget I asked."

"No, wait. You know I've never lied to you. I needed to be sure of what I feel. I do love you, Virgil. Please believe me. I'm not toying with you." But he didn't light up with pleasure at her words. He just looked at her with sadness. "Why are you so reluctant to believe me?"

"Because nobody loved me except for my father. I can't imagine that someone would love me now."

"Nonsense. You know that Lottie does, in a different way of course, but she cares a lot about you. And Tom considers you part of the family. No, there must be more that makes you so obstinate as to reject me."

He took a deep breath before saying, "I'm afraid. I'm afraid that it's a dream and it can't be real. And if by a miracle it is real, then I'm going to lose it, like I lost my father and the ranch, which were the only things that mattered to me. One day, I'm going to wake up again, alone in a world where nobody cares and I have nothing."

"But you can't live your life in fear. Take what

you have now, enjoy, be happy now. Sure, there will be plenty of times for unhappiness in the future. That is life. Grab what you can, what happy moments you have now. The ranch is yours. That is a fact." She opened her arms wide. "I am yours, if you want me. Do you?"

"Oh Brie," he exclaimed and caught her close to him, burying his face in her flowery smelling mane of dark hair. "Put that way, I can't say no."

She laughed. "I'll have to work on your enthusiasm. But it will do for now."

Outside it had stopped snowing and a sun-setting beam was making its way through the clouds. In the corral, someone had brought a wild mustang, which was prancing and snorting, sending puffs of white steam in the frigid air.

"He's gorgeous," Brianna whispered, barely daring to breathe. "Let's go see him."

The ranch hands and the family were gathered outside the fence surrounding the corral. Billy was perched on Tom's shoulders to see better, while Wyatt was pulling his grandfather's hand to come closer. Sam Donovan had to assure him that they had such horses in Texas too.

"Yo, Travis, why don't you show us how it's done in rodeo?" Tiny Pete called to his friend tongue-in-cheek.

"I am a bull rider, not a bronc rider. And in rodeo, I have to ride for only eight seconds." Travis said eyeing the wild horse with caution. "Besides, my days of riding wild animals have ended. I'm retired."

A tall cowboy came from the barn carrying a saddle.

"Oh, no." Brianna panicked. "Chris, you idiot, don't do it." But the cowboy was too far away and he couldn't hear her anyhow.

"Wait, look at him," Virgil pulled her back. "He knows what he's doing."

They watched him talking to the horse, raising his hand slowly to the horse's nose and after three feeble attempts to bite him, the horse let him touch his nose. His ears moved and he stepped closer to smell the stranger.

"Virgil, do something. He intends to ride the mustang," Brianna looked at him worried.

"Just watch. The horse is frightened, but he is or was used to the saddle."

Slowly, still talking to him, Chris raised the saddle and set it on the horse's back. The horse stepped back and neighed his displeasure, but calmed down when Chris talked to him. Just as easily, in one flowing motion, Chris vaulted into the saddle. He signaled to Cory to open the gate and then the rider and his horse were running away to freedom.

"Wow! He's good."

"He's a wizard."

"Let's see him bring the horse back," Travis grumbled.

CHAPTER 22

Dinner was over and the conversation flowed easily. Townsend and Sam Donovan were engaged in a chess game peppered with friendly banter about whether ranching was better in the colder climate of Montana or in the warmer, but drier and dustier, Texas.

After Lottie's good and abundant food everyone felt mellow, listening to Christmas music, while the fire logs crackled in the huge stone fireplace. In the bow window, a majestic pine tree twinkled with hundreds of lights. It was decorated with a lot of old and new, precious glass and hand made ornaments.

"I remember our great room with a similar fireplace, but after my father passed away, no one bothered to make a fire," Virgil said looking at the roaring fire.

Just then Cory came near him and whispered in his ears. "There's someone in the barn. You'd better come." And quietly went back outside.

"I'll be back," Virgil said and gently touched

227

Brianna's hair.

When he entered the barn, everything was quiet. He checked the stalls, but the animals were fine, the dogs were lying in the hay and the barn tomcat was licking its paws. A quiet winter evening.

"Is this a prank?" Was Cory drunk? Why was he playing juvenile pranks like this? The tiny hairs at his nape were raised and he had an inner warning of danger a second before he heard footsteps behind him. He turned.

"Unfortunately for you, it is no prank. It's real." His nightmare came alive and his stepfather stepped into the light. The years had not been kind with him. He had shrunk and was somewhat stooped. His eyes were bloodshot and his bulbous nose was red, showing signs of alcohol abuse.

He was a poor excuse of a human being, but unfortunately he also had a gun in his hand. Virgil cursed himself for being a fool, forgetting to take precautions. But who goes into the barn armed?

"What, cat got your tongue?" his nemesis asked

and cackled with a strident laughter at his own joke, exposing his yellow teeth. "You have never been much of a talker, brat. I guess you don't have much in that ugly head of yours." He laughed again.

It was good that he was confident, thinking Virgil was the same powerless kid he had been. Virgil could jump into the next stall and grab the fork he'd seen there. With luck, the old fool might miss his shot.

"Come, you have always liked to dawdle, but I don't have time. You know why I'm here. That attorney thought he could steal from me what is rightly mine. I slavered all my life on that ranch, enduring your mother's melancholy and ugly face."

"I understand you sold what you could and brought the ranch to ruin," Virgil said, trying to distract him, but the armed hand never wavered.

"Lies, all lies. The years were difficult. The weather didn't cooperate. The last cattle were killed in a blizzard right before they were to be sold."

"You wanted to sell cattle in winter?" Virgil asked. Every rancher worth his salt fattens his cattle during summer and sells them in the fall.

But the older man was caught up in his own reasoning. "And the mining prospect didn't show any promise. That land is worthless."

"Yet, you want it, even if by law and in truth it is not yours."

"I earned it. Do you hear me? It's mine and I'm going to sell it to the highest bidder," he shouted. "Maybe you'd like to buy it from me. I'll ask a pretty penny, I warn you." The idea seemed to cheer him up.

"Don't count your chickens yet. It is not yours."

"If you die, then it will be mine," the stepfather affirmed with conviction.

Virgil crossed his arms over his chest. Did this old fool imagine that he could acquire the ranch through murder and get away with it? "I have a fiancée and I willed all my worldly possessions to her, if anything happens to me."

"You didn't."

"I sure did. My uncle, the lawyer, recorded the will."

The old man seemed taken aback, but kept the gun pointed at Virgil. "You'll sign it over to me. Now."

"Why should I do it?"

"Because I have something you want."

It was Virgil's turn to be surprised. What could the old man have?

Still holding the gun steady, his stepfather searched his pocket with the other hand. He got out a tiny thing and threw it on the dirty floor at Virgil's feet. Virgil looked down. There in the dirt was his mother's cameo, her most precious possession, a wedding gift from his father. He remembered how every Sunday after dressing in her best clothes, she attached the cameo brooch to the shirt at the base of her neck.

Virgil squatted down to pick it up and look at it. Memories of happy times flooded his mind.

A click sounded in the silence of the barn. He raised his eyes. His stepfather was pointing the gun directly at his head.

"I've always imagined this. To have you again on your knees at my feet. To beg my forgiveness, to be at my mercy." An unholy glee lit up his eyes. An insane laughter echoed in the barn.

A shot rang out. The old man's gun dropped to the ground several feet away and he cried cradling his hand.

At the entrance, like an angel of vengeance, Brianna raised the rifle again. "Don't move or I swear I'll shoot your knees next time. I'm an excellent shot I warn you. And stop acting like you're hurt. I aimed for the gun. Your hand is fine."

"Who are you?" the old man's voice trembled when Brianna came closer.

"I'm his fiancée, Brianna Gorman."

"You're the rancher's sister? Why on earth would you choose a man like Virgil?"

"Because he is …perfect, good, hard-working, and generous. He's perfect and he's mine. I love him," she said her love showing in her eyes and in her voice.

The sneaky stepfather pulled out a knife and pressed it to Virgil's ribs. "Drop the rifle, girl. And get out of the barn or I'll kill this one here, your perfect fiancé," he spat.

This Virgil could handle. A loaded gun in the hands of a crazy fool was more risky. This kind of fight was easy. He could easily twist the arm with the knife; not to mention he could apply a quick clip under the chin to send him sleeping for a while. He was even relishing the fight.

But he didn't get to it. The old man rolled his eyes and his knees buckled and he dropped like a stone at Virgil's feet. Behind him, Lottie was checking her cast iron frying pan.

"Lottie." Brianna hugged her sister-in-law. "How did you know what was going on here?"

"The boys alerted me that the bad man had come back to hurt Virgil." Lottie nodded satisfied that all was well.

"Honey, you are lethal with a frying pan. Remind me to be careful in the future," Tom said from the barn door. He didn't mention that he'd almost had a heart attack when he saw his wife tiptoeing behind the criminal. "Let's get you back to the kitchen where it's warm. I'll need to have a talk with the boys about where they stick their noses and to whom they should report in such cases." Then he turned to Virgil. "Could you please tie him up until the sheriff comes? Cory had called him half an hour ago. He should be arriving by now."

This year was one of the most memorable Christmas celebrations everyone at the Diamond G ranch could remembered.

Early in the morning, the little boys came downstairs squealing with delight when they saw the pile of gifts under the tree. In a whirlwind of wrapping paper, ribbons and bows, the many presents they received where admired, tried on, and played with, and not just by the kids.

In the bunkhouse, the men were dressing up for the occasion. They too were invited at the ranch house to see what Santa had left for them under the tree.

Tiny Pete looked at Travis and whistled. "A new suit. Are you going to church again?"

Travis nodded satisfied. "Yep. I'm going to get

married."

Tiny Pete looked horrified. "Widow Krammer got her claws into you? Did you know about this, Angel?"

The mountain man didn't get to answer because a Tinkerbelle-like laughter sounded from the door. "Not Widow Krammer, but me," Maggie waltzed in, dressed in a white velvet dress under her jacket.

Everybody gathered at the ranch house where, with the same joy like kids, they received presents from Lottie's hands. As every year, she had some neutral extra gifts for the occasional visitors for Christmas. The lawyer from Montana received a nice warm wool scarf in the right navy blue colors that he liked. Maggie had received her gift earlier and was wearing the beautiful white velvet dress.

After the gifts were distributed and enjoyed, they all went to church for the Christmas service, followed by the wedding ceremony. The church was full when Maggie entered on Virgil's arm, who gave the bride away to an anxious looking Travis, worried that she might change her mind in the eleventh hour. Tom was best man and Lottie was matron of honor.

The women present cried appropriately and the entire congregation swore they'd never seen a more beautiful wedding or a couple more in love.

EPILOGUE

After the New Year

Widow Krammer went to the grocery store, where she ran into her cousin Phyllis Wade, who grabbed her hand conspiratorially and pulled her behind an isolated island of canned fruits.

"I need to tell you what I heard. All in confidence, of course."

Widow Krammer bent closer. "Of course. You know I don't talk to anybody and I don't spread gossip."

"I know. Although regardless of how careful we are, this news will spread soon all over town. I heard that Brianna Gorman, that wild girl who ran away to Denver last year, now she did it again."

"She went back to Denver?"

Phyllis looked around her and then whispered. "No, no. It's much, much worse. She ran away to Las Vegas with one of the ranch hands. She might have marriage in mind, but I doubt that once there, he'll see more than the slot machines." She pursed her lips and nodded to stress the importance of what she said.

"She left with Tiny Pete?" Widow Krammer asked alarmed. She still had tender memories of that particular cowboy.

"I don't know anyone tiny on that ranch, but it was with that homely foreman, Virgil Something."

"Ah," not Tiny Pete then. Good. The widow was relieved. There was still hope he might remember her fondly too.

"I bet she'll come back with regrets like before," Phyllis continued. "Too bad her brother took her back after she left the family to bear the shame," she added with righteousness.

If she'd bet, she'd have lost.

In fact, Brianna came back in the summer for a short visit. The news spread through town that she and her husband Virgil Townsend owned Bar T, a large ranch in Montana.

Brianna radiated happiness telling her family about the beautiful ranch house that she'd just finished decorating. She expected them all to spend the next Christmas in Montana. Her goats were very cute and productive and the first cattle they'd bought were doing well. Brianna had finally found her place in the world.

She loved her husband and by the attentive way Virgil hovered always near her, it was clear that she was the light of his life.

"Virgil, aren't you afraid of wearing your heart on your sleeve?" his brother-in-law, Tom asked him later on, when they were having coffee in his office.

Virgil smiled his lopsided smile and answered, "No. What's the point of love if not to show it?"

* * *

Keep reading for an excerpt from 'Trapped On The Mountain', book 3 of the *Wyoming Christmas* series:

VIVIAN SINCLAIR

Trapped On The Mountain

VIVIAN SINCLAIR

PROLOGUE

Twelve years ago

"Chris, wake up. Chris." His mother's voice seemed very far away, although she was near him, shaking him for good measure. He opened his eyes to look at her. "I swear you sleep like a log. The fire alarm sounded and you slept through it. Get up. We have to move, now. Pack your things. People are still confused by the fire alarm and we have to go. I don't have money for rent this month."

He packed in the bed sheets the few meager things he possessed, grabbed his old guitar, and followed her outside, where people were still debating if it was safe to return to their apartments or not. The scene was like a silent movie for him, a lot of action, but very muted sounds. He looked at his mother's car and realized that she was talking to him. He placed his bundle and his guitar on the back seat and got in.

"Where are we going?" he asked.

"Sheridan. I know a girl there who might give me

a job at a hair salon."

Ah, back to Wyoming. Too bad they had to leave. He really liked this small Nebraska town. He was a senior in high school and he would have liked to graduate here. Not that he had many friends. He was a loner. Eh, well, Wyoming would be just fine.

His mother was talking again, but he couldn't make much sense of it. It was like a swarm of bees were buzzing nearby.

He was tired. "Mama, I can't hear you. I've not been able to hear well ever since I was sick last month with that nasty flu. Maybe a doctor could help."

"Not now, Chris. I don't have money and we have no health insurance. You'll hear just fine."

But there was no improvement. After a few years, when he was working in an auto shop and had his own health insurance, the doctor fitted him with hearing aids and told him that was the best he would ever hear. Not much.

CHAPTER 1

Twelve years later, Diamond G ranch, Wyoming

The horse stopped and shook his head snorting, releasing puffs of steam through his nostrils in the frigid December air. It had been an exhilarating ride. Chris raised his eyes to the sky and laughed. Here in the open spaces of the Wyoming plateau he felt free. He patted the mustang on the neck. The ranch hands said it was a wild mustang, but Chris knew he had been broken to ridding and was used to the saddle. Probably he was still somewhat wild and too much to handle for his owner, so he had been released into the wild again.

"You are a great horse. You and I will get along famously," he crooned to the horse. The horse's ears twitched and he moved his head up and down. "Rightly so." And Chris laughed again. He rubbed his hands. It was cold. It was time to return home. Strange how he thought of the ranch as being his home now.

He remembered when he first knocked on his

brother's door, five years ago.

He was still mourning the death of his mother. He had a good job in an auto shop and the first thing he did when he got health insurance was to get his mother checked by a doctor. Her cough had worsened along the years and she was thin and feeble. There was nothing the doctors could do to help her at this late stage. Only then she relented and finally told him the name of his father, a cowboy passing through Cheyenne. He had decided to go and meet him. He had been a young man of barely twenty-four, curious to meet his father for the first time.

He remembered that day with precise details like it was yesterday:

It was a nice summer day with blue sky. It was warm even early in the morning. Chris had driven from Cody, where he lived, to Laramie, and then to the ranch. His father was one of the wealthiest ranchers in this corner of southeastern Wyoming. Not that Chris expected anything from him, not even to admit to fathering him in a one night stand passing through

Cheyenne. He was not sure himself if he wanted a father at this point in life. He was curious, that's all. He needed to understand better where he'd come from.

He was aware that his sudden presence - at his father's door and in his settled life - would be not only unexpected, but maybe even undesirable. He was prepared for everything, including being rejected.

He knocked on the door and waited, looking around. There was a lot of activity in the yard and quite a lot of ranch hands, sign of a prosperous business.

The door was opened by a pretty brunette young girl, who smiled, placed a Stetson on her head and marched outside calling behind her, "There's another one here." She went sauntering to the barn, leaving the front door wide open after her.

Not knowing what to do, Chris poked his head inside looking at the great room with a massive stone fireplace and comfortable chairs in front of it. From the hallway to the right, a man came to the door. He was tall and well-built, about Chris' age.

"Yes, what can I do for you? I think not much,"

he said, answering his own question. "Sorry, but I have all the ranch hands that I need for the season. I hired the last one a couple of days ago."

"I'm not here for a job," Chris answered, taking the measure of this man who could be related to him – by blood at least, if in no other way. "I'm looking for Tom Gorman."

"Well, you found him, but as I said…" the man said bending to brush some dirt from his jeans, with his hat.

"Could you please look at me when you are talking? I need to read your lips to understand what you're saying," Chris explained calmly.

This gave the other a pause. He straightened and looked at Chris. "You can't hear?"

"I hear some. I have hearing aids, but I prefer to read lips to be sure of what is said. About Tom Gorman. I was told he should be in his early to mid fifties, so it can't be you."

The rancher frowned. "That would be my father. He was named Tom Gorman also. But news travel slows in your corner of the world. My father died several years ago. What's your business with him?"

Chris was prepared for anything from surprise to rejection, but the news that his father had passed away left him deflated. It was anticlimactic. The confrontation he'd expected all his life was not going to happen, not now, not ever.

"Who are you?" Tom asked.

Chris waved his hand. "I'm Christopher. I'm his son. But it doesn't matter now, does it?"

Tom's jaw dropped in shock. Then he shook himself and pulled Chris in. "You'd better believe it matters. You don't come here and drop such a bomb, and then walk away like nothing happened."

"I didn't come to stir trouble or to ask for anything. I was just curious. That's all."

"A little late in life. Why now?" Tom asked, conflicted between interest and suspicion.

"My Ma passed away recently. Although I have asked her all my life who my father is, she refused to answer until she felt her end near." Chris shrugged. "So I came. It was a natural curiosity to meet the man who fathered me, nothing else."

Tom scratched his head, thinking. "Tell you what, we're going to town right now."

And so they drove to Laramie, to a lab, were they gave some samples for DNA testing.

"You'll stay with us until the results are back. Do you know how to ride?" Tom asked driving back to the ranch.

Yes, Chris knew very well how to ride horses. One summer, his mother hired on as a cook on a ranch. Unfortunately, she didn't know how to cook to save her life, and she was fired by the end of summer. But that summer was magical for Chris. He discovered that he loved to ride free on the range and that he had a special affinity for animals. He liked to spend time alone talking to them. It was the best time of his life. Like all good things, it ended too soon and they were again gypsies on the road, searching for another temporary place to live.

Back at the ranch, Tom and Chris saddled up and rode away. And Chris felt the same feeling of freedom, raising his face to the sun, and inhaling deeply the fresh, unpolluted air. He gladly helped to hammer posts for the fence, to string the barbwire, and to spread extra feed for the cattle in a remote pasture. There was not much time to talk and no one commented on his hearing impediment.

At the end of the day, his strained muscles protested, unaccustomed to a full day in the saddle. The girl, Brianna, gave him a jar with awfully smelling liniment that helped a lot and advised him to take a hot bath in the soaking tub.

"I didn't come here to ask for anything." He wanted to assure Tom in the evening, after they ate a plateful of beef stew, made by Mariah, the foreman's wife. "I have a good job in Cody, where I live. I work as an auto mechanic."

"Even if the DNA test confirms that you are our brother, the problem is that there is nothing I can do," Tom explained. "Dad left the ranch to me and some money to Brianna. The land is not to be partitioned or sold. There is no extra money. The ranch was not in good shape when Dad passed away and I worked hard these years to make it more prosperous. It will barely make a profit this year."

"I understand. No, I don't want your money." Chris had seen how hard Tom worked together with his men.

"However, if the results of the DNA test show you are a Gorman, then I would like you to change your name to our family name. Also, until the results come back, I expect you to work the same as us, to pull your weight. I saw you can work well without complaining. I like that."

The results came in two weeks and they proved without a doubt that good old Tom Gorman had fathered another son while passing through Cheyenne and Tom, his son, could not ignore his brother.

By then, the long hours of working on the range had honed Chris' muscles, and he loved everything, the land, the horses, the ranch, and his newly discovered brother and sister. He was loath to return to the smelly auto shop in Cody.

"Stay," his brother told him. "You are part of the family. The ranch is mine legally, but if you work as hard as you did until now, then you'll get a third of the profit at the end of the year. To be honest, it's not much right now. But it will grow in time."

"Thank you," Chris said and stayed at the ranch.

TRAPPED ON THE MOUNTAIN

To find out about new releases and about other books written by Vivian Sinclair visit her website at VivianSinclairBooks.com or follow her on the Author page at Amazon or on GoodReads.com

Virginia Lovers Trilogy - contemporary romance:

    Book 1 – Alexandra's Garden

    Book 2 – Ariel's Summer Vacation

    Book 3 – Lulu's Christmas Wish

A Guest At The Ranch – western contemporary romance

Maitland Legacy, A Family Saga Trilogy - western contemporary romances

    Book 1, Lost In Wyoming – Lance's story

    Book 2, Moon Over Laramie – Tristan's story

    Book 3, Christmas In Cheyenne – Raul's story

Wyoming Christmas Trilogy – western contemporary romances

    Book 1 – Footprints In The Snow – Tom's story

VIVIAN SINCLAIR

Book 2 – A Visitor For Christmas – Brianna's story

Book 3 – Trapped On The Mountain – Chris' story

Seattle Rain series - women's fiction novels

Book 1 - A Walk In The Rain

Book 2 – Rain, Again!

Book 3 – After The Rain

Storm In A Glass Of Water, a small town story

Made in the USA
Lexington, KY
21 February 2018